D1711532

COMFORT ZONED

ALLISON SPEKA

COMFORT ZONED

Cover design by Ashley Santoro

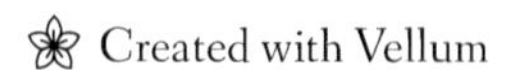

For all the readers who thought they would never be writers.

ONE
AL

"Are you serious?" I asked, gawking at my roommate, Jess.

She rolled her eyes at me in response. She just announced that she would be moving in with her boyfriend at the end of our lease this month, and I'm sure she was annoyed that I wasn't over-the-moon happy for her.

"Al, seriously, stop being dramatic. Tom and I have been together for a few months now, and it makes sense to take the next step. I know we've lived together since college, but, like, we both need to move on and try something different." She sighed, running her fingers through her thin dirty-blonde hair. "Look, I'm not trying to be insensitive, but it feels like we're attached at the hip sometimes. I need space to explore this relationship."

"I didn't realize I was weighing you down." I picked at a loose thread on the plush couch we were sitting on.

"Stop. Don't even go there. I didn't mean it like that." Jess's eyes softened as she looked over at me. "Look, I still love you, and I'm sure we'll hang out a ton. I'll be so sick of Tom after the first few weeks I'll be begging you to hang out and let me spend the night."

Now it was my turn to roll my eyes. I doubted that would be the case. In their five short months of dating, Jess and Tom had spent nearly every night together. If anything, I had been trying my best to avoid being the third wheel. That was why it felt like a slap in the face to hear her say that the two of us were inseparable.

Sure, that had been the case at one point. We met in college and did everything together. Parties, study sessions, cheap spring break trips to Florida. Growing up, I never had an easy time making friends. So when someone as lively as Jess took me under her wing on our first day of freshman orientation, it felt like I could finally breathe.

Gone were my anxieties about how I would manage to survive the next four years. She was the extrovert to my introvert. While I struggled to engage with new people, she thrived in every social setting. She was the reason I had any friends at all. Although, the only friends I had aside from her were more like acquaintances. I would see them at parties and gatherings Jess would coordinate, but I rarely saw any of them on my own.

Jess was my rock. My comfort zone. We had lived together every year in college and this past year after graduation. So even though she had been ditching me lately to hang out with her boyfriend, the idea of her moving out terrified me.

Should I move out on my own? Then I would never get out and see anyone.

Should I get a new roommate? The thought of living with anyone else made me physically itchy.

My spiraling thought process was making my head pound.

"I'm happy for you," I finally said. I plastered the most believable smile I could manage onto my face. "Tom is a great guy, and you're right, we have lived together for a long time. This was going to happen eventually."

She threw her arms around me. "Thanks, Al. I really am so happy."

My heart wasn't in it as I returned her embrace. It hurt that she'd waited to tell me this so close to our lease ending. I only had a few days to figure out what the hell I was going to do. And if I'm being absolutely, completely honest...I didn't love Tom.

It was a betrayal of Jess's trust to even think that about him, but I knew that the two of us would never be friends—or even interact—if it wasn't for Jess. We had nothing in common, so most of our conversations led to us discussing the weather. Occasionally, he would poke fun at my lack of a dating life while I waited for Jess to intervene. Tom loved video games, drinking, sports, and activities that involved a combination of drinking and sports.

The painful memory of being forced to join a beer-in-hand kickball league a few months back surfaced immediately. I did not possess any athletic ability, so it came as no surprise that during one game when it was my turn to kick, I missed the ball completely and fell on my ass, spilling beer all over me. Everyone got a good laugh out of that and joked about it the rest of the season, Tom leading the charge, of course.

So, yeah. Tom was kind of like the big, loud, jerky older brother that I never wanted. I had to admit he seemed committed to Jess though, perhaps his only redeeming quality.

"Okay," Jess exclaimed, jumping off the couch. "I'm off to Tom's. I'll probably spend the next few days there helping him sort through all of his crap so we can make room for mine. Let's hang out this weekend though. It'll be like our last goodbye hoorah." She pumped her fist. "Eric and Tiff are throwing a housewarming party. Let's go together."

"Cool."

Tiff was our RA when we were freshmen in college. She had been a senior at the time and acted as an older sister to us as Jess and I made one bad decision after another. I'll never forget the night I tried rum for the first time. Tiff held my hair back for hours. When she brought me coffee and aspirin the next morning, she never even mentioned how disgusting I must have been. After she graduated, the three of us kept in touch.

Although she was closer to Jess, Tiff had consistently gone out of her way to be kind to me. I didn't know her boyfriend, Eric, too well except for the few times Tiff had invited us to dinner at his restaurant. He was older than us, and we'd never had much of a real conversation. But he always footed the bill for our dinner, and he had my respect for that.

Jess lingered at the door, seemingly sensing my uneasiness over the life-altering bomb she had dropped on me.

"Love you, okay? This is going to be a good change."

The fake smile barely stayed glued to my face as she left the room. What the hell was I going to do?

TWO
DEAN

"What do you think of this for the new signature drink menu?"

A light pink liquid flowed out of the cocktail shaker and into a crystal glass I had already set out on the mahogany bar.

My business partner, Eric, grabbed the glass and took a small whiff before sipping my concoction.

"Damn, Dean. That's delicious." He swiveled around in the barstool he was perched on. "Hey, Sarah. Come give this a try."

Sarah tossed her red curls over her shoulder as she sauntered over to us from the host stand where she had been wiping down menus. She was our head waitress and had been with us since our restaurant, Luna, opened three years ago.

"What is it?" she asked, pursing her cherry lips as she leaned in to inspect the drink.

"I'm calling it the Luna Lover." I winked at her.

She eyed me as she brought the glass up to her mouth, taking a slow, seductive sip.

"Mmm. Yummy." Licking her lips, she set the glass back down. "Love the name."

She returned my wink before walking back to the front of the restaurant. From the slow way she swayed her hips, it seemed like she expected us to appreciate how good her ass looked in the tight black dress she was wearing.

Eric whistled under his breath.

"I know I'm a happily taken man, but remind me again, why you aren't getting with that?"

I groaned before grabbing the remainder of the drink and downing it. "I'm trying not to repeat old mistakes."

Back when Sarah first started, we slept together a few times. She made it clear she was looking for a commitment. I made it clear that I wasn't. All in all, it made for an awkward few weeks at work. Ever since then I've done my best to try to keep my distance—well, aside from that one time at last year's Christmas party. I'll be damned if it wasn't hard to resist flirting with a woman that looked that good.

Once at the front, Sarah turned back toward us and caught my eye. She gave me a coy smile before I ripped my eyes away, feeling guilty for being caught staring.

Fuck. I was not doing a great job at keeping things professional.

Eric smirked as if reading my mind. "Seems like that's working out really well for you."

"Shut up." I threw the bar towel I was holding at his face, but he dodged it, laughing.

"By the way, have you had a chance to look over the listings from the realtor I forwarded to you?"

The smile dropped from my face. "Eh, not yet."

"Dude, I need you to get on that. Our investors are expecting us to open a second location. I have a call with some of them tomorrow, and I need to tell them something."

I nodded while scratching the back of my neck. The

lingering feeling of being an imposter tugged at the back of my mind.

Eric and I met almost twelve years ago when I got a job at the country club where he and his family were members. I had just turned eighteen and was desperate to get away from the small neighboring town I had grown up in—and my miserable excuse for a father.

I had started as a busser and worked my way up to a barback. Eric would pop in whenever he was visiting from college. He always treated me with respect, and we became friends over the years despite our different upbringings.

By the time he graduated, a position was primed and ready for him as the manager, overseeing the restaurant and event space of the country club. Pretty much as soon as he started, he promoted me to bar manager. I felt a little uncomfortable at first. Like I hadn't earned my new position and he was just a friend doing me a solid. But Eric assured me time and time again that there was no one more qualified for the job.

After six years of long nights and working my ass off, I decided I was dying to go into business on my own, convinced I had what it took to open up the hottest restaurant and bar in town. That was the birth of Luna. For the most part, I was right. Luna became an overnight success, but unfortunately even with success came bills. I was up to my neck in debt and struggling to find a way out.

That was when Eric swooped in and saved my ass. I brought it up over drinks one day, and he immediately stepped in as my partner, set up meetings, and found us the investors we desperately needed. Even though I had helped make this place a success, I would always feel like a failure knowing I'd needed Eric's money to dig me out of a hole.

At one point it would have been my dream to branch out

and open a second location. Now, I couldn't help but feel undeserving.

"Dean, hey?"

Shaking my head, I tried my best to rid the negative thoughts from my mind. Eric was still in front of me and trying to get my attention. "Sorry, man. What's up?"

"I was reminding you about the housewarming party Tiff and I are throwing tomorrow night. You're going to be there, right?"

Shit. I had completely forgotten about that. While Eric was one of my closest friends, I didn't always love spending my time with some of the trust-fund types that tended to flock to him.

"Of course. I'll be there."

"What about Jared? I mentioned it to him during his shift yesterday, but he said he might have plans."

Jared was my best friend. We had grown up together and remained inseparable to this day. So much so that I even got him a job at the restaurant when he had fallen on some hard times.

"Why don't you ask him yourself?" I replied as a guy almost as tall as me with spiky blond hair sauntered through the front door.

Eric waved my old friend over.

"What's good?" Jared extended his fist for each of us to bump it.

"We were talking about the party I'm throwing tomorrow night. Can you make it?"

"Shit, Eric. Sorry. I totally forgot we got a gig for tomorrow. A wedding band backed out at the last minute, and the groom happened to have heard us play before. It would be huge for us if we could get more fancy events like this. The pay is great."

"That's awesome, Jared." I smacked him on the back.

He had played guitar and sung for as long as I'd known

him. Recently he'd gotten some friends together to form a band. Music had always been a passion of his, so I was pumped to see it working out for him.

"Speaking of weddings." Eric leaned into the bar, motioning for Jared and me to do the same. When our foreheads were practically touching, he whispered, "I'm going to ask her to marry me tomorrow. That's what the party is for."

My cold heart thawed, and my hand clasped around his shoulder as I gave him a lighthearted shake. "Congrats, man. It's about time."

"That's great, dude. Tiff is the best."

Eric beamed at the mention of his longtime girlfriend. They met years ago when she had a part-time summer job at the country club. She was a few years younger than us, but since we'd worked together, I knew her well too. She was the most genuine, kindhearted soul I had ever met.

"Maybe you two will finally get your act together and have dates by the time our wedding rolls around," Eric joked.

"Things with Janelle have actually been going pretty good. I could see this going somewhere," Jared responded.

At that remark, I scoffed. "If by going somewhere you mean to your bed for a few more weeks before you get sick of her, then I'm sure it *is* going somewhere."

"Just because you're Mr. Anti-Romance doesn't mean we all are." Jared shoved me good-naturedly. "Speaking of romance, tell me more about the big proposal, since I won't be there to witness it."

Eric looked like he was on cloud nine as he continued rattling off every detail about where he'd gotten the ring and how excited he was to see Tiff's face. I nodded and tried my best to smile along with him, unable to imagine the happiness someone could feel permanently binding themselves to someone else like that.

THREE
AL

My dark hair bounced right above my shoulders as I shook out my waves. I scrutinized my appearance in the small folding mirror that sat on my desk. Large brown eyes, dark lashes, tan skin, minimal makeup. Beautiful had always felt like a reach for me, but I had recently been growing more comfortable in my skin.

Standing, I walked over to the floor-length mirror on my closet door. Two dresses and one flouncy top already laid crumpled and cast aside on the floor. I had already resigned to wear my typical uniform of dark ripped jeans and combat boots. An oversized black band tee was calling to me, but I heard Jess's voice in my head telling me that I never dressed sexy enough.

"Screw it," I mumbled to myself as I pulled on the shirt. It was a casual night at a friend's house. Who was I trying to impress?

We were going to Eric and Tiff's house tonight, and I knew from years of experience that it would still be a while before Jess was ready. I pulled out my laptop to do some more apartment hunting. Given the late notice, there were hardly any acceptable rentals left in the Chicago area. So far all I had found was a shoebox studio that only had one window and cost way more than I wanted to pay.

It's not that I couldn't afford it. I had a great job—by great, I meant slowly crushing my soul and will to exist, but it did pay well.

Money was always tight growing up. After my deadbeat dad left one day to move across the country with a cocktail waitress, it was just my mom and me. She worked so hard as a nurse, always picking up extra shifts to ensure we could make ends meet. This was the reason I was such a frugal person. Jess would call me a cheapskate. Still, even though I knew I could technically afford the studio apartment, it was hard to stomach shelling out two hundred dollars more than what I was paying now for something so small.

On a whim, I decided to check Craigslist, hoping to find some nice older lady that didn't know how to use the apartment search engines—or the value of her rental. Scrolling around on the map view, I came across a posting in my current neighborhood and clicked on it.

> "Roommate needed immediately for 4 bedroom, 2 bathroom house. Available bedroom is very spacious with great light! You'll also have access to the furnished living room, dining room, kitchen, and patio. We are 3 young adults—men and women, so all are welcome here—that enjoy movie nights at home, going out, and having roommate dinners! We don't often host parties in order to keep our space clean and livable. If you are a tidy, relaxed twentysomething who is not an asshole, please reach out and we can schedule a time to meet!"

I clicked through the pictures. The house looked stunning. High ceilings, oversized rooms drenched in light. What a dream. Feeling daring, I grabbed my phone and shot off a quick text to the phone number provided.

> Al: Hey! My name is Al, and I'm reaching out regarding your roommate-wanted ad. I always clean up after myself, enjoy food and movies, and I haven't been told I'm an asshole in at least a few years. If the room is still available, I would love to set up a time to see it.

Grinning from ear to ear, I set down my phone. It was completely unlike me to reach out to a stranger like that, and the excitement of the unknown was giving me a buzz.

"Cheers!" Jess shouted as we all clinked our shot glasses.

The tequila burned as it traveled down my throat. I winced and frantically reached for a lime.

"You always make the funniest shot-taking faces." Tom chuckled as he bent down and kissed Jess on the mouth. The stolen kiss quickly turned into a make-out session.

Feeling awkward, I looked away. It wasn't uncommon for the two of them to partake in major PDA.

After a few long seconds, Tom broke away from the kiss. Still looking at Jess, he said, "Al, what are your plans now that I'm stealing your girl?"

"Well." I gulped some water. "I've got a few leads. There aren't many apartments available on such short notice, but I did find one studio that I'm seeing tomorrow. I also found this Craigslist post for a room for rent in this beautiful house with a few roommates. I doubt it's still available, but it's in such a good area—"

Jess snorted, cutting me off. "No offense, but you're the last person I can picture sharing a house with a bunch of people you don't know."

I shrugged, feeling deflated.

"Yeah, you really aren't great with new people. You hardly talked to any of my friends when we all played in that kickball league together," Tom agreed.

I scowled at him. "It's not like your friends made a huge effort to get to know me other than to constantly remind me what a klutz I am."

"Oh my God, I almost forgot about you falling on your face. That was freaking hilarious."

Tom roared with laughter while Jess snickered and shot me an apologetic glance.

"Sorry, Al, we're not trying to give you a hard time. It's just that you've always been a little uncomfortable around new people. Even in college I always had to drag you out and introduce you to people."

"Trust me, I know. But isn't that all the more reason to try to branch out?"

"I guess..." Jess trailed off, sounding unconvinced.

"Look, if you want to spread your wings, we'll be here cheering you on." Tom chuckled while ruffling my hair, a move he must know I hated. "And we'll also be right here ready to catch you when you fall."

"Thanks. I feel so supported." Sarcasm oozed from my words.

"Let's do another shot before we leave." Jess started pouring tequila, clearly hoping to break the tension.

"Cheers to our new place and Al growing up." Tom clinked his glass on the table and then against mine.

"Cheers," I jeered at him before downing my shot.

We arrived at a townhouse in Old Town twenty minutes later.

"All right, a plant that they'll kill in a week, check. Kind of nice wine that we found in the discount bin, check. Let's do this." Jess knocked a few times on the door before opening it.

Music and conversation spilled out onto the street as the three of us stepped inside. It looked like a decent showing with about fifteen people there.

Everyone looked older and nicely dressed in outfits that looked like a stylist put them together. Must be friends of Eric. I was pretty sure he was well off, and judging by this new house and the crowd he kept, I assumed that I was right. I looked down at my ensemble. What felt comfortable at home now made me stick out like a sore thumb.

Shit.

As if sensing my discomfort, Jess leaned in and whispered, "I told you to dress nicer. Why don't you ever listen to me? I swear I should have burned all of your T-shirts when I had the chance."

I shot her a dirty look before continuing into the house.

Their place was one of those towering new builds, with a rectangular design and an open concept. It was decorated tastefully in various shades of gray with a few conscious pops of color. We walked farther into the living room, smiling at a few familiar faces on our way to the kitchen. Aside from Tiff's sorority sisters we had met a handful of times, I recognized no one.

"Y'all made it," Tiff squealed as she spotted us. She threw her arms around Jess and me before giving Tom's arm a quick squeeze. Eric stood behind her and smiled at us. Maybe it was my imagination, but he seemed a little on edge. A far cry from the handsome, suave guy I was used to seeing when he was running the show at his restaurant.

We all shouted greetings simultaneously and complimented their new house before Tiff was pulled away to greet a new guest that had walked in.

Eric cleared his throat. "Please, help yourself to some drinks." He gestured toward a bar set up next to the dining table.

"Don't mind if I do." Without hesitation, Tom went to pour himself a drink, dragging Jess along with him.

I stood there awkwardly in front of Eric for a moment before trailing behind them.

There was a tall guy already at the bar making a drink. His large frame blocked half of the petite table, so I was unable to squeeze in next to Jess. Impatient, I waited for my turn. I was feeling self-conscious and looked forward to the burning taste of vodka to settle my nerves.

Between Jess and the stranger, a few bottles of beer were chilling in an ice bucket.

Better than nothing. I snaked my hand in to grab the coveted drink.

Just as I was about to make contact with the elixir, the man in front of me spun around suddenly and I was met with the clearest green eyes I had ever seen.

"Whoa there," he exclaimed in surprise.

Not expecting someone to be standing directly behind him, he nearly walked right through me. His body smacked into mine with almost enough force to knock me to the ground. He grabbed me by my shoulder with one hand, steadying us both.

"Sorry about that. I didn't see you standing down there."

My cheeks flushed at the mention of my short stature. True, I only stood at about five foot three, but that was a pretty standard height in my book. It wasn't my fault he towered over almost everyone here.

"I imagine that happens to you quite a bit considering nobody here meets your eyeline," I retorted.

His eyes crinkled as he cocked his head to the side. "Are you friends with Tiff?" he asked.

I didn't miss his surprised tone, and my face reddened even further. Was he implying that I didn't look like I belonged here? I mean, technically I didn't look like I belonged here, but rude of him to point that out.

Crossing my arms over my chest, I glared up at him. "Yes, we're friends from college. How do *you* know Eric and Tiff?"

While I didn't fit in with the crowd, this stranger didn't either. He donned a fitted black T-shirt and faded jeans. His dark, almost black, hair was semi-long and wavy. Tattoos peeked out from his shirt and ran almost to his wrist on one arm. Not exactly the clean, buttoned-up look the rest of the crowd was emanating.

He gave me a lopsided grin as if knowing what I was implying. "Eric is my business partner."

The color drained from my face as I recognized him. I had only seen him maybe twice before, usually behind the bar at their restaurant. The dark, handsome stranger had never approached us, but Eric had pointed him out to us before.

Great, so this guy was gorgeous, older, and successful, and I basically just insulted him.

"Oh, sorry, I th—"

"Here you go, Al." Tom broke the tension by thrusting a glass into my hand.

He surveyed the man looking down at us and squared his shoulders, attempting to appear taller.

"Sorry, was our girl bothering you? She can be a bit abrasive if you catch her before a drink," he practically shouted.

"Shut up, Tom," I hissed, and snatched the clear liquid he offered.

The man smirked and was about to open his beautiful mouth to say something before Eric's shout cut through the crowd.

"Dean, come here a minute, will you?"

I couldn't help but think how much I liked the sound of his name. Dean gave us all an apologetic smile before squeezing by me to meet Eric in the living room, where the two started discussing something in hushed tones.

I groaned audibly. Why did I have a habit of making a terrible first impression?

FOUR
DEAN

"I'm freaking out, man," Eric whispered in a panic.

I clasped one hand on his shoulder, attempting to calm him down the best I could.

"It's going to be fine. One little question and then it'll all be over. You know she's going to say yes."

Eric scanned the room until he locked eyes with Tiff. The tension left his shoulders almost instantly.

He looked back at me with a gleam in his eyes. "Thanks again for coming. I know this isn't your scene."

Giving him my best supportive smile, I patted his shoulder and sent him off in the direction of his future betrothed. I couldn't for the life of me understand why he was getting all worked up over something so insignificant. It was no secret that I didn't believe in marriage, or committed relationships for that matter. It probably had something to do with the shitty example of love I experienced firsthand growing up. My dad was an emotionally abusive dick, and my mom let him walk all over her, and me, until the day she died when I was thirteen.

I took a swig of my beer and surveyed the crowd, waiting

for the inevitable squeals and frenzy that would happen when Eric finally made his public declaration of commitment to Tiff. Too bad Jared was busy tonight. He was usually my buffer at parties like this. That guy could talk to a wooden post better than I was able to connect with these people.

A group of girls talking in hushed tones glared at me from across the room, and I averted my gaze. I might have slept with a couple of Tiff's friends a while back. A sore subject between the two of us.

My eyes swept over the other side of the room before they fell on the girl with the small frame in the oversized T-shirt that I had bumped into at the bar. She stuck out in this sea of pastel crewnecks, and she appeared to know it, judging from the way she crossed her arms over her chest.

My head cocked to the side as I examined her. Although she was doing her best to hide her body, it was clear that she had a good one, especially her legs, whose outline I could see beneath her tight black jeans. Her face looked innocent and uneasy, but still undeniably beautiful. She had a tendency to wrinkle her small, sloping nose, which I already found to be adorable. She looked young though. Did she say she knew Tiff from college?

The loud, stout man that handed her a drink earlier was leaning into her and shouting something into her ear. I was trying to assess if it seemed like he was her boyfriend or not when, all of a sudden, the crowd erupted in cheers and the girl's face broke into the most stunning smile I had ever seen. I was so mesmerized by it I almost didn't realize I had missed Eric's proposal entirely. I tore my gaze away and started cheering with everyone else.

"Oh my God, I can't believe this," Tiff exclaimed as she bawled tears of joy.

Everywhere around me people lifted their phones to capture videos and pictures of the special moment.

Eric caught my eye, and I gave him a grin and a thumbs-up. Girls swarmed Tiff, begging to see the ring.

The abrupt change in the room had me feeling claustrophobic. Desperate for some space, I edged my way past the commotion to the bottom of the stairs behind the living room before taking them two at a time.

FIVE
AL

"I can't believe they're finally engaged. Did you know?" I asked Jess as we waited behind a few girls to congratulate the happy couple.

"Hope this isn't giving you any ideas," Tom interjected, pinching Jess's side.

Jess swatted his hand away and smirked. "I had a feeling. Tiff and I got our nails done on Wednesday. She said she didn't want to assume anything, but I know she was hoping it'd be tonight."

"Gotcha," I replied, feeling let down.

Jess and I were supposed to get drinks after work on Wednesday before she bailed at the last minute. Before I had a chance to mention that to her, we made it to the front of the line to talk to Eric and Tiff.

"Congrats, you two," squealed Jess as she threw her arms around both of them.

Tom also gave a hardy "Congrats" as he pumped Eric's arm in the most aggressive handshake I'd ever seen.

"Congratulations." I was too awkward to go in for a hug.

Tiff beamed before embracing me without hesitation. "Thanks, Al. It's always so good to see you."

"You too. I'm so glad we could be here." My cheeks hurt from maintaining my smile, and I tried my best to hide my discomfort. I nodded at Eric, hoping he didn't also try to hug me.

Eric noticed my stiff demeanor and took a half step back before yelling, "Who wants a shot to celebrate?"

Almost everyone cheered in response as Eric broke out a bottle of tequila that probably cost more than my entire grocery budget for the month. Shot glasses were passed around, and I knocked back mine quickly, hoping to feel anything other than a strong sense of not belonging.

After the second bottle of tequila was opened, the party loosened up quite a bit. Music was now blasting out of the house's very expensive surround sound system. Jess and I were singing along to a song that was popular when we were in college, and Tiff and her sorority sisters were right next to us, bopping along. I was feeling great and comfortable in my own skin for once, a perk of alcohol that I needed to see a therapist about.

As the song ended, we all giggled and caught our breath.

"I'm going to find a bathroom," I yelled to Jess.

"Okay," she responded before jumping up and down in excitement as the next throwback song came on.

"You can use the one upstairs!" shouted Tiff over the music.

I flashed a smile of gratitude before stumbling over to the

stairs. I hadn't realized how much I'd had to drink until I was concentrating on every step I took to reach the second-floor landing. Upstairs led to a hallway with several closed doors. After a moment of hesitation, I decided to try the first door on my right. I staggered through the threshold before realizing that it was an office—not a bathroom—and that someone was sitting at the desk.

"Oops, sorry." I tried to back up quickly, but unfortunately my klutziness was in full effect when I was tipsy. I backed right into the edge of the open door, and pain shot up my spine.

"Oof, ouch," I groaned, rubbing the afflicted area.

A soft chuckle floated over to me from the desk, and I was reminded that I wasn't alone. To my horror, Dean was getting up from the desk chair and walking toward me.

"Are you okay?" he asked as he stopped a foot from the door.

I couldn't help but think how nice his voice sounded. Deep and smooth. He should have his own podcast.

"You have a nice voice," I blurted out.

He tilted his head to the side, and his lip tugged upward in an amused smirk.

My cheeks flushed as I realized that I had said that out loud.

"I—sorry. I did—" I stammered before snapping my mouth shut. I took a deep breath through my nose, trying to collect myself before continuing.

"Are you apologizing for complimenting my voice? I hardly think that's necessary."

My face burned. Between the tequila and my embarrassment, I'm sure I resembled a tomato by now. I took one more deep breath, collecting myself.

"No, of course not. I was apologizing for barging in here. I was just trying to find the bathroom," I said, doing my best impression of a calm person.

"It's down a few more doors." He pointed back toward the hallway.

I muttered a "Thanks" and turned to leave, but the two shots of tequila I had earlier pressured me to face him again.

"What are you doing here by yourself anyway? You know there's a party downstairs."

"It was getting a bit...crowded down there for me." He retreated to the desk chair and gestured for me to sit in the chair opposite the desk.

I did my best to confidently saunter over before plopping into the leather seat. My small frame was immediately overtaken by the plush cushion.

Dean grinned in response to what I'm sure was the least sexy position I could possibly be sitting in.

"If you aren't having fun, why not just leave?"

He let out a slow breath and leaned his elbows on the table, pressing his chin into his hands. "Eric's one of my closest friends. I had to be here to support him. Besides, he had some paperwork for our restaurant I needed to look over. Figured now was as good a time as any to do it."

"Your restaurant is really nice, by the way. It's a great spot."

His eyebrows shot up in surprise. "Have you been?"

"Just a few times. Tiff brought us there." I felt like a stalker for some reason.

He tilted his head and narrowed his eyes, assessing me. "You said you were friends with Tiff, right?"

I nodded. "We know each other from college."

He seemed unconvinced.

Now it was my turn to narrow my eyes. "What, you don't believe me?"

He chuckled. "Forgive me. You just seem a little...younger than Tiff."

I snorted and rolled my eyes. "If you must know, she was our—my and my roommate, Jess's—RA when I was a freshman. So, *yes*, she is a little older. But hardly."

I didn't know why, but the last thing I wanted Dean to see me as was some young, immature girl.

He looked like he was doing some mental math in his head. Desperate for him to stop obsessing about my age, I rushed to change the subject. "So, you're Eric's business partner. How do you guys know each other?"

Dean broke his concentration and leaned back in his chair. "Eric and I go way back. We met at this country club I used to work at. His family had been members for years and then he became a manager later on."

"That makes sense. Eric seems like the country-club type."

Dean's eyes went hard. "Eric might come from a wealthy family, but he's a great guy. He's saved my ass more than once."

"No, that's not what I meant." I scrambled to sit up in my seat, panicking that I had offended him. "I just meant anytime I've been around him I'm always afraid to touch something."

I looked around frantically.

"Like this," I said, pointing to a small boat inside a glass bottle sitting on the desk. "This is probably worth, like, half of my annual salary, and it's just sitting here ornamenting this desk."

Dean's eyes softened, and he relaxed. "You're probably right." He paused before continuing. "If I'm being honest, this isn't really my scene. I've never meshed with Eric's friend group. We've always just kind of kept our business and friendship separate from the life he grew up in. Anytime I come to a party like this, I always feel out of place."

I nodded. "I know what you mean."

He looked me up and down. My body grew warm with his intense gaze, and I started to play with my hair to break the tension I was feeling. This was easily the best-looking guy I had ever had this long of a conversation with.

"So you're here with your roommate—"

"Jess."

"And your boyfriend?"

I snorted before breaking out into a full-on belly laugh.

Dean smiled at my amusement. "So it's safe to say the loud guy with the intense handshake is not your man?"

I gasped for breath, trying to choke out a response. "Absolutely *not*. That's Jess's boyfriend, Tom."

"Ahh, Tom. Not a fan, I presume?"

My smile fell. "No—I mean. He's totally fine. He's great for Jess. I'm happy for them." I spouted off every robotic response I could think of.

Dean winked at me. "Our secret. I promise," he said before drawing a cross over his chest with his index finger.

"Thanks," I responded, relieved. "It's not that I hate him or anything like that. He's just...a little...not my type of person, I guess. But he seems to love Jess, and that's what matters."

"What is your type of person?"

Dean leaned forward as if he was actually interested to hear my response.

I hesitated. "Maybe I'm still trying to figure that out," I admitted.

"Well, I wish you the best of luck with that," he said, standing up and extending his hand. "I'm Dean, by the way."

"I know—shit—I mean, I'm Al." I jumped out of my seat and took his hand. It felt like electricity flowed from his fingertips, and butterflies formed deep in the pit of my stomach.

"Al," he repeated. "Is that short for something?"

"Alissa, but my mom doesn't even call me that."

"Got it. You strike me as more of an Al anyway."

His stare felt almost intimate with just the two of us up here.

"Well, Al. I better congratulate the happy couple and head out."

"Oh," I replied, completely failing to mask my disappointment.

He squeezed my arm as he brushed past me into the hallway. "It was nice talking to you."

"You too," I muttered as I watched him disappear downstairs.

I let out a frustrated huff.

Should I have been forward and asked for his number? I didn't often get crushes on guys, but Dean was insanely handsome and easy to talk to. Well, somewhat easy, but I'd take anything given my affinity for social awkwardness.

Whatever, it didn't matter anyway. He was way out of my league and obviously thought I was too young for him, judging by the look on his face when I said Tiff was my RA.

I sank back down into the plush chair and checked my phone for the first time all night. A notification signaled a new text message from an unknown number. My brow furrowed in confusion as I opened the text.

> Unknown: Hi, Al, nice to "meet" you! Sorry for the late reply. My name is Nora, and the room is still available. Are you free tomorrow morning around 9? You can check out the house and meet all of us to see if it's a good fit.

The room for rent. I had completely forgotten about that.

Emboldened by the alcohol and the doubtful words of my friends earlier, I typed back my response.

Al: 9 works for me! Text me the address.

I checked the time and saw that it was already almost midnight. Considering that my social clock was pretty much maxed out, I should probably call it a night.

SIX
DEAN

"Thanks again for coming." Eric threw his arms around me and embraced me.

"Wouldn't miss it for anything."

"Thanks, Dean." Tiff craned her neck to give me a peck on the cheek.

"I'll see you at Luna tomorrow. Don't forget to look over the new leases I sent you."

"You got it, boss." Little did he know I was doing exactly that while I should have been down here drinking and socializing.

I saluted Eric before turning on my heel toward the door. Before I could take a step, my eyes caught sight of Al and who I presumed to be Jess, arguing in the corner.

"I want to stay, Al. Just go by yourself."

"But almost everyone has left already. Can't we go home and make nachos like old times?"

"I'm staying at Tom's tonight anyway. Just go order a cab." Jess waved her off and turned away as if she couldn't be bothered to speak to her.

My blood boiled at the dismissive gesture. No wonder she had said something about still figuring out who her type of person was. This was apparently Al's roommate and friend, and she was treating her like shit.

"Hey, Al!" I shouted to get her attention.

Both she and Jess turned toward me.

"How does he know you?" Jess whispered, all of a sudden taking interest in her friend again.

I didn't give her a chance to respond to Jess. "I'm heading out too. Let me give you a ride."

"B-but you don't even know where I live."

I shrugged. "Doesn't matter. C'mon, let's go."

She walked over to me and gave me an unsure smile, no doubt questioning what my intentions were.

"That would be great actually. And thanks, Eric and Tiff, for having me. Congrats again."

"Of course. Thanks for coming." Tiff gave Al a hug and eyed the two of us warily.

"See ya around, Al." Eric nudged her in the shoulder as if she were a five-year-old kid and not a fully grown woman.

I stepped aside and gestured with my hand for Al to lead the way, but before she could take a step forward, Tiff shouted, "Wait!"

She grabbed Al by the arm and dragged her backward, whispering something inaudible into her ear.

I narrowed my eyes at Tiff, wondering what she could possibly have to say that couldn't be shared with the wider group. Eric looked between them and me and mouthed, "Women," at me, as if I was supposed to take something from that.

Seconds later Tiff released a flustered-looking Al, who ambled straight past me and to the door. I gave Tiff one final confused look before heading outside.

"It's the van right up here," I said, pointing to an old, beat-up Ford.

"A van in the city?" she questioned as we both got in.

"I need it for picking up supplies. Plus, I share it with my friend Jared. He's in a cover band."

"That's so cool." She fidgeted with her seat belt. "I love live music."

"You should come sometime. They're playing at the bar next door to Luna next Saturday."

She perked up at that. "I'd love to come."

I threw the van in drive and pulled out of the parking spot. "Where do you live?"

She rattled off an address that I recognized immediately as being in my neighborhood.

"That's right by me. See? I knew this would all work out."

I flashed her my best smile that I knew women found charming. To my surprise, she ducked her head to examine her hands that were folded in her lap.

What gives? Sure, she seemed shy, but I was getting the vibe that she found me attractive when we were talking in Eric's office.

"Am I allowed to ask you what Tiff said to you back there?"

Her brown eyes went wide as she looked back at me. "It's embarrassing."

I chuckled. "Embarrassing for you or embarrassing for me?"

She shrugged, but I noticed a smile start to play on her lips. "She told me to be careful."

"That's it? Be careful of what? I promise I'm an excellent driver. I can provide references."

She laughed softly, which sounded like music to my ears. "I don't think that's what she was worried about."

She looked to be in pain at the thought of telling me whatever it was.

I pressed. "What did she say?"

"Y'know..." Her voice trailed off.

Raising my eyebrows, I took my eyes off the road for a second to look at her. She was gesturing between the two of us with her hand, and I got the drift.

Ah, so Tiff was worried I would corrupt her little friend. This wasn't completely surprising, since I had hooked up with a couple of her sorority sisters back when she and Eric first started dating. I wasn't interested in anything more than a casual fling, something I was very up-front about. That didn't stop each girl from wanting more. It also didn't stop the next girl from sleeping with me despite all the warnings about me. What was it with some women thinking they could change a guy?

"I promise you, and Tiff, have nothing to be worried about."

Al slumped down in her seat, her full lips forming a soft pout.

"What's that face for?" I questioned.

"Do I have nothing to worry about because you don't find me attractive?"

I nearly choked from surprise at her bluntness. She seemed so shy yet so...not at the same time. Maybe I didn't have a good read on her yet.

"Look, anyone with eyes can see that you're attractive. I'm just not much of a commitment guy. Tiff knows this, which is why I'm sure she warned you not to get involved with me. But she, and you, have nothing to worry about. I wouldn't go there with one of her friends again."

"Again?"

I sighed in aggravation. "Look, it was no big deal. I just went on a couple of dates with a few of her friends. It didn't work out. They weren't happy about it, Tiff wasn't happy with me. End of story."

She considered this. “Like, a couple of her friends that were there tonight?”

I met her eyes and nodded.

“Was that why you were hiding out upstairs?”

“That might have been one of the reasons.”

She continued to stare at me, which was causing an uncomfortable tightening situation in my pants. I should change the subject, but I couldn’t help pushing it.

“Why doesn’t Tiff seem to think you can take care of yourself?”

“I guess because I haven’t had a ton of experience,” she said matter-of-factly. “I’ve never really had a boyfriend before, and the guys I’ve dated casually have never seemed all that interested in me. I think Jess is desperate for me to meet someone so I have someone else to hang out with.”

Her vulnerable answer surprised me. I wanted more. “Elaborate.”

“On what?”

“On these guys. Why weren’t they interested in you?”

She looked me up and down, as if not sure how much she wanted to share. “I guess you’d have to ask them. But…I know I can be a bit awkward. And quiet. I’ve never been great with new people, and it’s hard for me to…to open up.”

“It kind of feels like you’re opening up to me.”

“Maybe it’s because you seemed just as out of place at that party as I felt.”

I fought back the grin that was threatening to break loose on my face.

“Al, how old are you?” I asked. It was not a subtle change of subject, but I wanted to know.

“Twenty-three. Does it matter?”

I sucked in a breath. “No, it most definitely does not.” *Because I’m not pursuing this*, I added to myself.

Why the fuck was I pestering her about her age? It didn't matter. If I was just going to hook up with her, it certainly didn't matter, and I wasn't planning on dating her or anything like that. Still, a part of me cringed when she said twenty-three. She probably thought of me as old or washed up.

I pulled up to a large brick building.

"This you?"

"For now," she muttered. "Thanks again for the ride."

I waited for her to get out of the car, but she paused with her hand on the door handle.

"Can you maybe send me the details about your friend's show next Saturday? I meant it when I said I love live music."

Thrown off, I grabbed my phone from my pocket. "For sure. Put your number in."

She typed in her contact info and handed it back to me before exiting the van.

"Good night, Al."

She waved at me before heading inside.

SEVEN
AL

Downing my second cup of coffee, I checked the time on my phone.

8:15.

I had to be out of here in ten minutes to tour that studio apartment before checking out the room for rent.

Yesterday, the idea of living with three strangers sounded new and exhilarating. Today, it sounded like a smelly, over-crowded nightmare. Chalking up my excitement to the influence of tequila, I considered canceling. I wanted to live alone, and it was silly to waste their time. The studio would work out perfectly.

"Why are you up so early?" Jess groaned as she stumbled out of her room.

"Apartment tours. What are you doing here? I thought you were spending the night at Tom's."

"He decided to meet up with some friends after you left, so I decided to come back here instead."

This wasn't the first time Tom had ditched Jess to hang out

with his friends. Funny, since she was always ditching *me* to hang out with *him*. I thought about pointing that out to her, but she probably wouldn't see the humor in it.

"I'm going to die." Jess collapsed on the sofa and chugged the glass of water I had poured myself. "Spill," she said when she finally came up for air.

"Spill what?" I asked, playing dumb.

"You know what. Eric's hot business partner. The one who drove you home last night. What's his name again?"

"Dean."

"Dean. That's it. I knew I remembered Tiff talking about him. You know, back before Tom and I got together, she mentioned setting the two of us up."

Internally, I rolled my eyes. I doubted that happened, considering what Dean told me last night about his past with Tiff's friends.

"He seemed nice," I said, not wanting to give too much away.

Jess snorted. "From what Tiff said, he's anything but. She told me he's a major F-U-C-K boy. I think she was worried he was going to take advantage of our sweet, innocent Al." She squished my cheeks between her hands, and I batted her hand away.

"I'm not that innocent," I mumbled. In truth, I was pretty innocent. I had only slept with three guys, and it had all been pretty standard stuff. None of them looked, or made me feel, the way Dean had—and all we had done was sit in a car alone together. I shuddered to think how he would make me feel if we were doing other activities.

"Please, that guy would eat you alive."

"Whatever, Jess. He's way out of my league anyway."

"That's one thing we can agree on."

"What do you think? You can't beat this price if you want to live alone in this area."

"It's cozy," I replied as I looked around the small studio apartment.

It was pretty decent. I could be comfortable here. The apartment was a large twenty-by-twenty square with a kitchen against one wall and an open space to place a bed, desk, and a small table and chairs. I might even be able to fit a love seat in here if I configured the layout just right.

Not much to look at now, but with the right decorating skills, this place could be adorable. Unfortunately, interior design was not in my wheelhouse.

"Well, you better act fast if you're interested. I have a few more showings right after this, and I have to give it to whichever qualified application I receive first."

The realtor handed me an application and went over the deposit amount and rent one last time.

"Great, thanks. I'll head over to a coffee shop and fill this out right now."

He walked me out of the apartment, and I stood on the sidewalk, feeling utterly underwhelmed.

There was nothing wrong with the apartment. In fact, on paper, it met all of my criteria. I glanced at my phone to check the time.

8:56.

I had just enough time to walk over to the other house and meet these mysterious roommates I had already built up in my head. This morning I was so sure I wanted to live alone, but standing there in front of what could be my new home, I felt empty. Did I want to commit to this place, this feeling, for an entire year? An entire year where the chances of me doing something new and spontaneous went from slim to none?

My thoughts were interrupted as a young couple approached. I could hear them gushing about finding something in their budget as they squeezed each other's hands. The realtor I had just said goodbye to opened the door to greet them. He caught my eye as he escorted the couple inside and tapped his wrist as if to say, *Time is ticking*.

I checked my phone one last time before racing away.

A few minutes later, I stood outside of an old greystone. All of a sudden, I felt a slight sense of panic. On an impulse I had rushed over here, most likely giving up the quaint studio to the eager couple behind me.

What if I hated these people? What if they hated me? What if the house looked nothing like the pictures?

Shit.

This was a mistake. An impulsive, self-indulgent, idiotic mistake.

I thought about leaving and filling out the studio application in case it was still available when the red door in front of me swung open.

"Oh, hello?"

A girl stood before me. I guessed this was the Nora I was texting with last night. She stood several inches taller than me and was wearing corduroy overalls. Her faded blue hair was divided into braids.

She looked me up and down, her eyebrows drawn together in confusion.

"Um, hi," I started. "My name is Al. I'm here about the

room for rent?" My words came out as a question. Did I have the wrong address?

Nora's pursed lips transformed into a beaming smile. "Oh my gosh, of course. Sorry, I'm such an idiot. When you said your name was Al, I thought you were a guy. I'm Nora. It's nice to meet you in person."

She extended her hand, and I walked up the three steps to meet her in the doorway before engaging in her enthusiastic handshake.

"Nope, definitely a girl. Sorry to disappoint."

"Oh no, not at all. There are already two men living here, and that's already way too many if you ask me. It's just like this constant den of testosterone and body sweat."

I forced a smile, still feeling uneasy.

"And I'm totally putting my foot in my mouth. I swear we're all really fun, normal people. Please come in, and you'll see that the place is clean and does not reek of male body odor."

Nora stepped aside and pushed the door open, inviting me in.

"Thanks."

I stepped past her and into a small entryway that opened up to a spacious and bright living room. The house was narrow and long. The hardwood floors extended from the living room to the dining room and kitchen. All three rooms were separated by partial walls with wood trim. Off of the living room, there was a staircase with a grand banister, which I assumed led to the bedrooms.

"Wow, what a beautiful place."

"Thanks. We aren't allowed to paint, so I've tried my best to inject some life into this place with as much wall art as I possibly can. Anyway, I've been here for two years now. It's funny, I actually found this place through a roommate-wanted ad originally. Cameron is the only one left from that original group. And Sean only moved in about a month ago when Lauren moved to New York. Now, alas, we've lost yet another roommate to a move—hence the Craigslist post."

"So this place is a bit like a revolving door of strangers?"

"Well, nobody is a stranger for long. I've met some lifelong friends here." As if we were already familiar, Nora threw her arm around my shoulder and led me into the living room.

"Let me give you the tour. This is the living room, where we spend many a night watching ridiculous reality TV." She continued leading me through the house. "And here we have the dining room, which I admit we don't use often, but we do try to do a family-style dinner once a week. Just past here is the kitchen. Through that door"—she gestured to a door with chipping paint next to the refrigerator—"is a very creepy basement that we only venture into when laundry must be done. Also, I should mention we have two kitchen rules. One: if it's labeled with someone's name, don't eat it. Two: clean your dishes immediately after use. None of that soaking bullshit in this house."

Just off the kitchen, there was a small room that appeared to be an old porch that was framed in. There was nothing inside except a massage table and a rug.

"Um, what's this?" I was nervous to hear the response.

"Oh, that's mine. I'm an artist at heart, but that doesn't always pay the bills. I do a lot of side gigs, including"—she pats the table—"massage therapist."

I must not have hidden my horror well, because she started backpedaling.

"I mean, I *hardly* have any clients, and usually they're only here when everyone else is at work."

This was a mistake. "Um, I'm not so su—"

"Oh, please don't let this scare you off. Cross my heart and hope to die, I swear you will never see a nude client."

"Great." Somehow I wasn't feeling comforted.

Nora smiled. "Do you have any questions before I show you the room and take you outside to meet the guys?"

I hesitated before responding, "Look, this seems like a great setup. And you seem so nice. But honestly, I've never lived with anyone before except for my best friend. I'm a little nervous about the lack of privacy."

"Oh, please don't worry about that. All of our rooms have locks on them so that yours can be your own peaceful oasis. And if this does work out, the two of us can share one of the bathrooms so you won't have to deal with all the obnoxious mini hairs the guys leave in the sink when they shave."

Sharing a bathroom with just Nora did make this whole arrangement sound a little more manageable.

Nora waved me upstairs to show me a surprisingly spotless bathroom and an empty bedroom. The room was small, but it had a window that overlooked the street. That might not seem like a lot to most, but considering that my current view was of a brick wall, the natural light made the whole space look almost ethereal. I could feel the tension in my shoulders easing as I surveyed what could be mine.

After the tour, Nora led me outside to a large concrete patio where two guys sat awaiting us.

One was quite tall with short black hair and frameless glasses. He was pretty cute, albeit rather serious looking. The second was a little shorter and very blond, wearing a tight gray T-shirt that showed off his toned arms.

The blond one jumped to his feet and smiled, showing off his blindingly white teeth.

"Hi, I'm Cameron, Cam, whatever you want to call me. It's

nice to meet you." He went right in for a hug, and my entire body stiffened. I was not a hugger.

"Oops, sorry," he said, releasing me. "I'm terrible with personal space. Don't worry, it will not happen again unless we've been drinking."

The taller one stood up and waved awkwardly. "Hey, I'm Sean. I know it's weird that we're just creepily waiting out here for you, but we've found that it works best when just one roommate does the initial vetting process."

"Right. Um...hey. I'm Al."

"I'm so relieved you're not another guy," Cameron gushed. "We need more feminine energy around here."

"What a stupid thing to say," interjected Nora. "Al can give off whatever energy she wants to regardless of gender."

There was a quick pause as everyone took in my large T-shirt, black joggers, and Birkenstocks. Maybe I should have put a touch more effort into my appearance this morning, but in my defense, I was pretty hungover.

"No, that's okay. I hope I give off some amount of feminine energy despite my middle-school-boyish appearance," I joked.

"Stop, you're literally stunning," said Cam as he walked forward and took my face in his hands. "I mean, look at those gorgeous eyes."

"Cam, personal space!" shouted Sean.

"Shit, shit, sorry." He dropped my face and took a step back, holding his hands up like he had been caught committing a crime.

I laughed, feeling more comfortable by the minute.

"So, Al. What do you do?" Sean asked, sitting back down while also gesturing for me to take a seat in an empty chair.

"Ugh, could you think of a more boring question?" asked Nora, rolling her eyes.

"Um, I'm actually in data and analytics for a start-up downtown. It's okay, not my dream job or anything, but it pays the bills." That was an understatement. I loathed my job.

"Oh my gosh, another smarty-pants," exclaimed Nora while she nudged Sean's knee. "This guy right here is a big-shot financial advisor."

"I'm hardly a big shot."

"Don't be modest, Sean," Cam boomed.

Sean and I exchanged a knowing glance. I would never undersell my intelligence, but it was pretty common for people to fuss over what I did like it was rocket science or something. It definitely was not. "What do the rest of you all do?"

"Well, like I told you, I do a bit of everything," replied Nora. "Besides trying out the whole massage therapy thing, I waitress and bartend some nights, I walk dogs, I deliver groceries." She was lifting a finger each time she listed a new job. "But all so I can afford to work on my art. I have an online shop, and I'm trying to make money off it, but it's still a work in progress."

"Wow, that's amazing. Did you paint some of the pieces in the living room?"

"Tons of them. I'll give you an art tour later."

Cam cleared his throat to get my attention. Nora and I smirked at each other.

"Currently, I'm an executive assistant to the CEO of a public relations firm," he said. "She's absolutely fabulous, but also a nightmare. Think *The Devil Wears Prada* but slightly more realistic. It's just a stepping stone though. I'm trying to get on the front lines of PR. Manipulating a story to fit a narrative that suits me is my favorite pastime."

As we continued to make small talk, I weighed my options. After my initial panic subsided, I actually found myself quite comfortable here. Yes, these people were strangers, but they seemed normal enough. And if I didn't make this move, I'd likely wind up a complete recluse.

In the end, they extended me an offer to move in. To my surprise, when I said yes, I only had the teensiest bit of anxiety about it.

EIGHT
DEAN

I gnawed at the tip of my pencil as I walked around the expansive pantry taking inventory. How many bags of pasta had I counted? Shit. I shook my head as I mentally started tallying them again.

My mind kept wandering to the previous night and driving Al home. Conversation with her had come easy. And not the bullshit fake charm conversation I usually had with girls. There was something about her that made me want to talk to her again.

Shaking my head, I tried to rid my thoughts of her. She was friends with Eric's fiancée. Plus, she was way younger than me. There was no way I'd be interested in something serious, so it was inevitable that I would wind up disappointing her in the end.

Still, something about her awkward sincerity had my hand itching to send her a message. I'd had every intention of deleting her number, but when I watched her walk away from my van, I didn't have it in me. Now it stayed there in my phone, tempting me.

"Hey, boss." Jared strolled in at that moment, completely interrupting my already scattered thoughts.

"Shit, I lost count again," I muttered.

"Let me." Jared grabbed the notebook from my hand. "Shouldn't you be out there talking to Eric anyway?"

He was right, which was why I was hiding back here doing a job I typically pawned off onto someone else. I wasn't ready to have the tough conversation Eric was sure to force me into.

"How was your gig last night?"

"It went great. Even gave our contact information out to a few engaged couples. I'm telling you, man, I think we could have a really good thing going with this whole wedding band thing."

"That's awesome, seriously. I'm proud of you."

Jared rolled his eyes and smacked the clipboard against my chest. "Don't get all sappy on me, D. That's so lame."

"I can't help it. It's exciting to see my oldest friend succeed."

"Well, you better be there to watch me succeed next weekend. Don't forget about the show we're playing next door. And make sure to invite everyone you know. We're more likely to get invited back if we bring in a good crowd."

I chewed on the inside of my cheek, thinking of my promise to text Al the details.

It would be an unnecessary complication, I told myself. If I were to invite her, I would have a hard time resisting her. There were plenty of other people I could invite. People who were better suited for a casual fling.

At that moment Sarah peeked her head through the pantry door. "Dean, Eric is looking for you. He's in the back office."

"Tell him I'll be right there," I said. I started to turn away before snapping my head back to face her. "Hey, what are you doing next Saturday? Jared's band is playing. You should come."

"I know, he already invited everyone on staff that has that night off." She gave me a slow, sultry smile. "But if you're specifically asking *me* to go with *you*, the answer is yes."

With that, she gave me a wink and retreated from the doorway.

Jared side-eyed me, looking unimpressed.

"Don't start."

"What was that about? You've said a million times that you're not into her, and you know she's still pining after you."

I cursed under my breath. Asking Sarah like that had been a mistake. I was too caught up in trying to prove to myself that I couldn't care less about Al and the fact that she was off-limits.

"I'm going to talk to Eric," I muttered before leaving Jared behind to finish the inventory.

"I'm going to need your final answer on these properties. You've had weeks now to review them."

Eric sat across from me in the small office we shared at the back of Luna. It was more of a closet that we had converted by gutting the shelving and hooks and replacing them with a small desk plus a few chairs. Five packets of paper outlining different properties for rent sat on the desk between us.

"I think we should go with the one in my neighborhood," I said matter-of-factly, pointing to the packet closest to me. Eric was right. I had been dancing around a decision. But ever since looking at the lease options again at his party, I had been thinking nonstop about the best choice. I wasn't going to let the fear of failure, or my insecurities surrounding finances, get to me any longer.

"Look, this area used to be all college kids. Lately, with the new construction going up everywhere, an older crowd has been moving in. This is our chance to be one of the first nicer restaurants in the area. But we're still reasonably priced, so we won't scare off any of the people that have been around awhile."

Eric picked up the papers and flipped through them, considering what I had said. "I know that our investors were leaning toward the one downtown, but I think you've got a good point. I'll call the realtor and have them send over the final lease for us to review."

"Just like that? You don't want to discuss it more?"

"Dean, I'm sick of you doubting yourself. I trust your judgment. This place wouldn't be what it is today if it wasn't for you."

"You mean if it wasn't for your money."

"Stop bringing that up every time you're feeling self-loathing. Yes, I was able to help you out with investors. Yes, I took on a management role. One I would say I'm pretty damn good at, if I do say so myself. But you're the visionary behind this place. I couldn't have done jack shit if you weren't the brains behind this operation. Luna would have failed a long time ago if it wasn't for you."

After his outburst concluded, I blew out the breath I had been holding. Deep down I knew he was right. That it was wrong to doubt myself. It was hard though. Growing up, the person that should have been supporting me and lifting me up did nothing but bring me down and make me feel worthless.

"Thanks, man." I still couldn't meet his eyes. "I appreciate you saying that. I know I've got to work on my confidence."

"Damn right you do." Eric smirked and went back to reviewing the packet.

"Knock, knock."

I swiveled around in my chair to see a vision of pink, Tiff, standing in the doorway.

"Hey, babe." Eric jumped to his feet and greeted her with a peck on the cheek.

"Are you almost ready to go?"

"Just about." Eric started collecting some of his belongings. "Tiff and I are having dinner with our parents tonight to celebrate the news."

"Have fun, you two."

Tiff stared at me, clearly wanting to say something but withholding.

I raised my eyebrows as if to say, *Go on.*

"So you drove Al home last night..."

I groaned, already over this conversation.

"Yeah, how did that go?" Eric asked, wiggling his eyebrows mischievously.

"Nothing happened, all right? Give me some credit. I just drove her home."

Tiff shifted from foot to foot. "I'm sorry I'm being so weird. It's just that Al is such a sweetheart, and she's always struggled to get close to people. Maybe it's because we met when I was her RA, but she feels like a little sister to me or something. I don't want to see her getting taken advantage of. She doesn't deserve that." She looked at me pointedly. "And she doesn't have enough experience to fend off the likes of you."

"*Me?*" I scoffed, and gestured to myself.

She rolled her eyes in response. "You know how you are. Just lay off my friend, okay? There are plenty of other women in this city. Take your pick."

With that, she turned on her heel and motioned for Eric to follow her.

"Yeah, dude. Listen to my girl," Eric said, louder than he needed to.

When he looked to ensure Tiff had her back to him, he winked and mouthed, "Go for it," before turning to follow her.

NINE
AL

"Did you already sign something? I bet we can get you out of this. Who knows what kind of people they could end up being. Or what they could be hiding. I can't even think about you living in such a place."

I took a large inhale as I listened to my mom panicking on the other end of the line. The train car I was sitting in was surprisingly empty considering that it was 8:30 AM on a Tuesday.

I loved my mom, but she tended to fuel the flames of my anxieties instead of extinguishing them. We didn't talk often, mostly because she was constantly working. We didn't see each other often either, since she still lived in Michigan where I grew up. Sometimes I wished we were closer, especially since she was the only parent I had. But she single-handedly provided me with a stable childhood, a fact I would be eternally grateful for.

"Mom, I told you. I'm excited about this. They all seemed really welcoming, and the house was beautiful and felt so full of life. I think it's time I tried something different."

"Is this because you're worried about living alone now that Jess is moving out? I know it can be scary, but I don't think the solution is finding a bunch of strangers on the internet. You know you have such a hard time making friends."

I inhaled again, practicing my yoga breathing.

It was kind of true. Growing up, I didn't have a single friend to my name. Even though we didn't have a ton of money, my mom enrolled me in a private school for the ultrarich. I had received a scholarship for my academics, and she thought it was some sort of miracle that I'd be able to get such a good education.

It was evident early on that I didn't fit in. Even though we wore uniforms, my classmates always found a way to show off a new trend or an expensive fashion piece. The girls in my class would gush over the designer shoes and backpacks they wore. My beat-up white tennis shoes did not pass their test.

No one went out of their way to bully me or anything like that, but there were many parties I never received an invite to. I never went to a high school dance because I was never asked. All in all, I was pretty much invisible. It was such a relief when I went off to college and met Jess. She was so bubbly and friendly and immediately took me under her wing. Unfortunately, the sting of rejection from my younger years still lingered with me now.

"It's not that. Living alone would be great. I wouldn't have to see people on a daily basis, and I could be a hermit and stay in as often as I liked." I started fiddling with the strings on my backpack. "The problem with living alone is that I know without Jess dragging me to things, I would completely isolate myself. I'm so sick of struggling to make new friends and feeling like I'm always just glomming on to whoever I meet through Jess. I feel like I'm not even a whole person by myself."

There was a short pause on the other end. "Of course

you're a whole person. You have friends and an amazing job. You don't need to prove anything to yourself or anyone else."

"Thanks, Mom," I mumbled, getting off the train at my stop. I started walking the two blocks to my office. "Hey, I'm about to be at work. I'll talk to you later."

It was so hard to talk about not feeling happy with my mother. In her eyes, I was successful and popular. I couldn't seem to explain to her that something was missing. That I wasn't fulfilled. Sure, I liked my friends, but I didn't fully connect with them. Probably a by-product of only meeting people through Jess. As for my job...well, I couldn't stand it. I was doing way more than my title implied and not getting even a fraction of the recognition for it. Just because I wasn't a suck-up, I seemed to always get overlooked in meetings.

I rustled through my bag for my ID card. After scanning in, I walked through the turnstile and toward the elevator. When I arrived at my desk, my manager, Shelley, was already there leaning on my cubicle's half-wall divider.

"Good morning. How was your weekend?"

"It was great." The corners of my lips strained to turn upright, and my cheeks felt heavy to lift.

"I'm stopping by because I want you to review the new dashboard that Trent is rolling out. It's going to give us such good insight into our marketing spend."

"I actually helped him build that," I said firmly.

By "helped him build that," I meant I took his shell of a dashboard that didn't even function and created visuals, added filters, connected a new data source, and generated several new metrics. I felt blindsided that he sent it out for review without even cc'ing me on the email. We had discussed presenting it together, but it was typical of Trent to "forget" to include me.

She looked uncertain. "Ah, well, that was nice of you to

lend a hand. I'd still like for you to QA the final result just to make sure there aren't any bugs."

There weren't any bugs because I built it myself and already triple-checked. "Sure, I'll get right on that."

After plugging away for a few hours doing some mindless data entry, I went back downstairs. Jess and I were grabbing lunch, something we did semi-regularly, since we both worked downtown.

As soon as I stepped outside, I regretted not grabbing my jacket. Even though it was mid-September we were already getting chilly days intermixed with warm ones.

Arriving at the restaurant, I scanned the tables to see if Jess had already sat down. After spotting her in a booth near the back, I plopped down across from her.

"Hey, stranger," she greeted me. "How's the grind?"

"Literally miserable already."

"You're always so dramatic. It's only been a few hours."

"Well," I challenged. "Upon entering the building, before I could even turn my computer on, I found out that Trent is once again taking credit for something I helped him work on. Not even helped, I practically built the thing from scratch. So my day has been pretty much downhill from there."

"Ugh, stupid Trent. He brings nothing to the table except audacity."

Jess was well informed about Trent, my only teammate, as I frequently liked to vent about his antics over lunch and happy hours.

We ordered our food, and Jess started talking about the rest of her weekend with Tom and preparing for the move. Apparently, they had gone out and bought new kitchenware together.

From the way she was glowing, you would have thought they had gone ring shopping.

"What about you, Al? Did you sign that studio? I know most of the furniture is mine, but I'd be happy to sell you some things, since Tom already has some nice stuff of his own."

At that moment the waiter arrived with our food, which saved me from giving an immediate answer. Telling Jess about my soon-to-be living situation was not something I was looking forward to.

"I'll only need my bedroom furniture. I ended up signing a lease agreement with those people from that Craigslist ad I told you about. I went to meet them yesterday, and they were all pretty cool, so I decided to go for it."

Jess froze mid-bite, gaping at me. "You what?"

"I know it's surprising, but I meant it when I said—"

"'Surprising' is the understatement of the century," Jess cut in. "I can't believe you did that. They're probably going to murder you in your sleep or something."

"They're completely normal." For some reason, I already felt defensive of my new roommates.

"Of course they *seemed* normal. They need to lure you into their trap before they can reveal who they really are."

"You're ridiculous."

She grilled me about my new roommates for a few more minutes before redirecting the conversation back to herself and Tom. Eventually, we paid for our food and stepped back outside together. We were about to wave goodbye when Jess stopped and turned toward me.

"Oh, I almost forgot to ask about Dean. Did he ever text you?"

"Nope." I frowned, not trying to hide my disappointment. "He did mention inviting me to his friend's gig on Saturday though."

"Jared's gig? Oh yeah. Tiff invited Tom and me to that, but we can't make it."

My cheeks grew hot with annoyance that Jess had already secured an invite and seemed to know Dean's friend on a first-name basis.

"You know Jared?"

"Not really. He bartends at Luna. I've talked to him before when I've gotten drinks with Tiff."

Now my eyes were also burning at the mention of Jess and Tiff hanging out without me again. It seemed like it was becoming a pattern lately.

"Oh" was my only response.

"Well, hopefully Dean texts you, but I wouldn't hold your breath. Judging from what Tiff has told me, that guy is only interested in one thing." She looked me up and down. "You're probably not his type anyway. I bet he goes for more leggy blondes that wear short skirts. You know the type."

With that mood-boosting comment, we parted ways.

It hadn't been that long since I gave Dean my number, so I was still stupidly holding out hope that I might hear from him. Jess was right. There was no way I was his type. It was silly of me to be so forward. I had practically forced him to take my number, and now it was clear he never wanted it.

"Stupid," I muttered under my breath.

My cheeks flushed with embarrassment as I thought about how I had fantasized about him texting me and declaring that he could not stop thinking about me. Daydreaming about guys was easier than actually dating them.

At that moment I resigned myself to stop thinking about Dean. It was a silly crush that wouldn't amount to anything. I needed to get my head out of the clouds and start focusing on real connections.

I was sick of feeling so alone.

TEN
DEAN

My knee bounced up and down on the floor as I stared out the window of the slow-moving train car. I was running late for something yet again. It seemed to be a trend for me this week. Normally, I tried to make work-life balance a priority, but it was impossible now that we were finally following through on opening a second location.

After Eric and I decided which building we wanted to rent, we were able to sign the paperwork and occupy the space immediately. The spot had great bones. It used to be a popular coffee shop a while back, but it had sat vacant for at least a year. It helped that it already had a working kitchen and a great layout. Most of the work that we needed to do was cosmetic.

An unforeseen con of the great condition of the building was that our investors were chomping at the bit for us to open in a month. We had tried numerous times to tell them that it was going to be impossible, but they simply shoved more money in our faces and expected that we would get it done.

My phone buzzed in my pocket, and I pulled it out to see another text from Sarah, asking me what I was doing tonight.

Shit.

This was the third unwarranted message this week. Normally, I might have been tempted by her flirty advances, but right now all I could think about was work, and her forwardness was starting to irritate me. I admit, I messed up asking her to go with me to Jared's gig on Saturday. My hope that she would forget about that now seemed unfounded.

When the train arrived at my stop, I raced the few blocks to the modest courtyard building I called home. After being at Luna all day, I only had a few minutes to run in and change before heading to the new spot to do some work. I had promised Eric I would pick a paint color yesterday—I didn't—and get the supplies in place for the contractors to start work this evening. Eric and I had done a lot of cleaning this week and even some light demo, but it was time for the professionals to take over or we'd never finish in time.

Rushing inside in a frenzy, I barely registered that there was already someone else here, feet propped up on my coffee table like they owned the place.

"Jared, I told you I was busy tonight."

I rushed by him without a second look and threw some leftovers from the restaurant on my kitchen island.

"Food if you haven't eaten."

"Thank you much." He got off the couch and started sifting through what I had brought.

"Ugh, you know I don't like salmon."

"I didn't bring it for you."

"So disappointing," he grumbled while grabbing a fork and shoveling in bites. "You want to go out tonight?"

"I can't. I need to go to the hardware store and pick up some stuff for the contractors."

Jared groaned his disapproval. "You've been working

nonstop this week. I'm sick of it. It's Friday night, for God's sake. You deserve a night off."

"I'll be taking a night off tomorrow, remember? I'm being a supportive friend and going to your gig, even though I have a million other things I could be doing."

Jared grunted in response.

Ignoring him, I circled around the island, making my way to the bedroom at the end of the hall. I proceeded to rip through my dresser and grab an old pair of jeans and a hoodie before emerging back into the living space.

"Are you going already?"

"It's five. I told them I'd have the stuff there already."

"Okay, okay. Stop begging. I'll go with you."

Jared grabbed his sweatshirt off the couch and followed me.

"Fine, but you're not allowed to get distracted in the store."

"But, Dean, you know I love to look at power tools," he whined in response.

ELEVEN
AL

I hit save on a document I was working on before closing my laptop for the day. It was Friday afternoon at the office, and everyone seemed to be discussing their weekend plans, judging by the increasing volume of conversations.

They say preparing for a move is one of the top most stressful times in a person's life, but this week had felt pretty uneventful to me. Every day after work, I ordered takeout and organized my things into boxes while watching reruns of my favorite show. It sounded lame, but I enjoyed my little packing ritual. I was almost disappointed that tonight was the last night I'd be doing it.

Flipping my phone over, I pretended not to be disappointed when I didn't see a new unread message. I had been trying, and failing, not to check it all day. My first weekend without Jess and I had no plans. Was I that pathetic?

Oh well.

Rising from my desk, I threw my backpack over my shoulders. A group of coworkers my age, including Trent, were gathered by the elevator, laughing at some joke I missed.

"Hey, Susie, any exciting Friday night plans?" I asked one of the girls from marketing whom I was friendly with.

"Oh, not really. Just hanging out," she replied.

Everyone seemed to quiet down as we all piled into the elevator. I checked my phone one more time, but it was pointless.

As we arrived at the lobby, I walked out the main door first and started making my way to the train.

"Have a good weekend, Al," someone shouted from behind me.

I turned around. "You too."

When I looked back, I saw the group of my coworkers heading in the same direction, still laughing. I frowned, feeling a pang in my stomach. They must be headed to a happy hour nearby.

No one from work ever invited me to go to happy hour with them, and I couldn't figure out why. Sure, I didn't like Trent, but he didn't know that. I always went out of my way to be polite and helpful. And most of my other coworkers seemed cool when we chatted in the break room. I would have loved to get a drink with them.

Pushing them from my thoughts, I put my headphones in, blasting a playlist I had made earlier in the week.

Twenty minutes later I got off the train and popped into a hardware store that was en route. Last night I used up my last box, and I still had a few odds and ends that I needed to pack up.

Jess already moved the rest of her stuff, including all of the living room furniture, last night. She was supposed to do it on Saturday and help me move, but Tom had only been able to borrow his friend's truck last night.

I came home to an empty apartment, ate Chinese food on my bedside table, and tried not to cry reminiscing about old times. I wished I could have spent this last night alone with Jess, but it was clear that her priorities had shifted.

My cheeks started to redden, and I felt that familiar burning feeling behind my eyes. I hated that I was a crier. My mom used to joke that I was always so stoic and then, all of a sudden, the tiniest thing could set me off into a fit of tears. It was true, I didn't get emotional over stereotypical things. But sometimes my thoughts, or frustrations, overwhelmed me, and crying seemed to be the only release.

I scanned the box selection, debating which size to buy. There was a shadow looming next to me, and all of a sudden, I was very aware that eyes were on me.

"Al?" Looking up, I saw a tall, attractive man with messy dark hair in a black hoodie. Dean.

"Oh, um. Hi, hey. What's up?" I stammered. *Shit*, it was not as easy to talk to him without a few drinks in my system.

"Fancy running into you here. Are you mulling over a box purchase?"

"Oh, yeah," I replied, returning my gaze to the display. "Trying to decide if the large one is too large."

He chuckled. "And what would make it too large?"

"Well, in theory, a large box sounds like a good idea. I can fit more into each one, so I'll have to buy less. But if I do go with this one, I'll probably end up overstuffing it, and then it'll be too heavy to lift. So I'm thinking buying more medium boxes is actually the right move."

"Wow, I can see your conflict now."

"I think I've got it under control." I smiled up at him, grabbing the boxes. I awkwardly stuffed them under my arm and turned to face him.

"Are you moving or something?"

"Yep, I'm moving tomorrow."

He frowned, his brows creasing together. "Where to?"

"Just down the street. I live in this neighborhood now...oh, I guess you knew that. Duh. Anyway, Jess—I think you met her at the party, remember? She's moving in with her boyfriend—I think you met him too—so I had to find a new place."

I realized I was rambling, but I felt powerless to stop my word vomit.

"Glad to hear you aren't going anywhere far away," he said, flashing me a smile that made goose bumps pop up on my forearms.

"So," I said, trying to take the attention off of me, "what brings you to the hardware store on a Friday night? I'm sure you have better things to do."

"Not at all." The skin around his clear green eyes crinkled as he held up a few different paint samples. "I'm trying to pick a paint color. What do you think?"

I assessed the various shades of green he was holding. "I'm not great with this kind of stuff."

He leaned in even closer to me. "I want to hear what you think."

I bit the inside of my cheek and took another look.

"This one is nice." I pointed to a dark sage-green color. "I don't really know what look you're going for, or what room you're painting, so please ignore me if that's not the vibe."

He threw me an adorable, lopsided grin before lifting the color I had selected up to the light. "You're right, it's perfect."

"Oh, are you sure? I would hate for you to pick it just to be polite and then hate it when you see it at home."

"It's not for my house."

I gave him a puzzled look.

"It's for the new restaurant. Eric and I signed a new lease, and we're fixing the place up now."

"Your—a new restaurant?" I nearly choked. "Well, you should definitely get a second opinion, then. That's way too much pressure to put on my paint selection."

He laughed and looked back down at me before playfully smacking the top of my head with the samples he was still holding.

"You should stop second-guessing yourself." He looked at the paint card again. "Sea Moss will be the official color of Luna Two."

"Luna Two?"

"Not the most original name, but the investors want to make sure we're establishing our 'brand.'" He put air quotes on the last word.

"That makes sense. I love it." The last thing I wanted to do was make him think I didn't like the name. "Is Luna named after anyone?"

Dean smirked and looked at his feet almost self-consciously, if that were possible for him. "Eric's childhood pet."

I let out a short laugh that, to my horror, sounded more like a snort before snapping my mouth shut. "Shit, I'm sorry. That's not funny. It's a great name."

He grinned in response. "No, it is pretty funny actually."

I stood there in silence, searching my brain for something witty or flirty to say to keep the conversation going. Thankfully, Dean saved me by speaking next.

"Did you hire movers?"

"Nope, just doing it myself. It's just what's in my bedroom. It's not like I have any ridiculously heavy furniture or anything."

He looked me up and down. "Just yourself? What about the bed?"

"Um, well, I was thinking I could wrap it in a sheet and drag it out. I'm sure it won't be too bad."

He looked unconvinced. "I can't imagine your tiny little self carrying a mattress alone. Let's see your muscles." He gestured for me to raise my arm.

I gave him an exasperated look, since we both knew I had no muscles to speak of. "It's more about technique than manpower," I countered.

"And how will you be transporting everything?"

"I rented one of those U-Haul trucks."

Dean continued to stare at me. His green eyes searching mine.

"What?" I finally questioned.

"No offense, but I have a strong feeling that you're not a good driver."

He was teasing me, and I loved every second of it.

"Um, offense taken." I actually hated driving and had been told many times that being a passenger in my car was frightening. One of the great things about living in Chicago was that I could take public transportation everywhere.

"When was the last time you drove?"

"What's with the interrogation? Not that it's any of your business, but last year when I was home, I drove my mom's car to—"

"Last year?" Dean exclaimed, his eyebrows shooting up. "You don't own a car and you haven't driven in a year?"

"It's like riding a bike," I insisted.

"Are you able to cancel the U-Haul?"

"I mean, I guess. I didn't put a deposit down or anything. I know I'm not moving far, but I can't exactly lug my mattress a few blocks to my new place."

He hesitated, stroking his chin between his index finger

and thumb. "Cancel it," he finally said. "I can bring my van, and I'm going to help you move."

Stunned, I loosened my grip on the boxes, and they all fell to the floor. Before I could bend down to collect them, Dean beat me to it, tucking them under his arm.

"You really don't have to do that. I barely have any stuff. I'll be done in no time by myself."

"Then you'll be done even faster if I'm helping you," he insisted.

"Why would you want to help me? I'm sure you have something better to do on a Saturday morning."

"Actually, I don't think I could live with myself if I was at home, picturing you struggling to get a mattress twice your size into a truck you don't know how to drive." He laughed melodically, handing back the boxes.

A shy smile played on my lips. "Well, if you absolutely insist."

"I absolutely insist." He grinned at me.

"Dean, are you almost don–oh, hello. Am I interrupting something?"

A guy appeared at the end of our aisle and ambled over to Dean. Although he wasn't my type, he was handsome in his own right. He stood just a little bit shorter than Dean and had a tough edge to his face. Maybe it was the eyebrow piercing.

"Not at all. Jared, this is Al. Al, Jared."

Jared looked me up and down as if assessing me. "What happened to no distractions?"

"Ha ha." Dean fake laughed while gripping both of Jared's shoulders tightly. "Jared, why don't you wait for me at the checkout?"

"I'm good." Jared waved him off. "So, Al. How do you know my boy Dean?"

"Oh. I don't really. We met last weekend at Eric and Tiff's house."

"Your Tiff's friend, then?"

"Yep."

Dean was shuffling from foot to foot, and I could sense his discomfort. Was he embarrassed that his friend caught him talking to me? That seemed ridiculous, but he was no longer meeting my eyes and seemed desperate to get out of there.

Ugh, I wish I could disappear.

"You should come to my band's gig tomorrow. Ten o'clock at the bar next to Luna. Tiff will be there."

I snuck a glance at Dean, who seemed suddenly enthralled with the paintbrush selection to his right.

"Oh, um. Maybe. I've got a lot going on tomorrow."

"Please come. It would mean a lot to me."

I couldn't help but smile at Jared's feigned sincerity. "You don't even know me."

"I feel like we're old friends already."

At that, I finally laughed.

"For real though. It'll be a lot of fun, and the bigger the crowd, the more likely my band will get asked back."

"I'll think about it, promise."

"We better get going," Dean said, and gave me a half wave.

My face fell as he turned away. Before Jared got there, I could have sworn Dean was flirting with me. Guess I suck at reading people. So much for him helping me move.

Just as Dean was about to disappear around the corner of the aisle, he whipped his head back around.

"Uh, what time should I be at your place tomorrow?" he asked as soon as Jared was out of earshot.

"Oh—uh, nine? I kind of wanted to get an early start."

"I'll see you then."

"Wait, I'll give you the address."

"Al, I remember." He flashed me a smile and shook his head like he thought I was silly.

After he was out of sight, I smiled, pleased with myself. That feeling lasted all of thirty seconds before I realized that this meant he would be at my apartment tomorrow morning. Suddenly, I was a ball of nerves.

TWELVE
DEAN

"What was that back there?" Jared asked as soon as we had all of the supplies loaded into the van.

"Nothing." I avoided his eyes as I maneuvered the car out of the parking spot and back into the street.

He scoffed and looked out the window. "It didn't look like 'nothing.' Why are you being weird right now?"

"I'm not being weird."

"Dean, I've known you for twenty-five years. You're being weird."

Irritated that he wasn't going to drop this, I let out an exasperated sigh. "It's nothing. I just talked to that girl—Al—for a while at the party last week. She was cute and kind of endearing, but I promised Tiff I'd lay off."

"So you're trying to hook up with her?"

"No. I shouldn't. She's younger than us, and I didn't get the vibe that she wanted something casual. Tiff didn't seem to think so..."

"Eh, don't think about Tiff. Of course she's going to look out for her friends, but I'm sure this girl can handle herself."

"We're here."

Grateful for the excuse to drop the conversation, I pulled into a small parking lot that was attached to the older brick building we now leased. The bones were great, and the location was only a block off the main street, surrounded by apartment buildings. I could already envision twinkle lights lighting up the patio out front. This place would draw in young professionals like moths to a flame.

Hopping out of the van, I headed for the trunk to grab the supplies I needed to bring in. Jared followed, hot on my tail.

"Oh, before I forget, can I take the van home with me tonight? We'll need it to lug all of our instruments to the bar, and it would be easier than picking it up tomorrow."

I froze with two cans of paint in my hands. "Um, I kind of need it tomorrow morning. Can I drop it off after?"

Jared narrowed his eyes. "What, for more supplies? We can just get them now while we're already out."

"It's not that," I muttered.

"Then what?" he demanded.

"I'm helping Al move in the morning."

Jared looked at me, dumbfounded, before bursting out into a belly laugh. "Wait, let me get this straight. You're helping that girl back there—the one you don't even know if you're interested in—move tomorrow?"

I shrugged my shoulders.

"You. The person who has no free time at all right now is going to use up precious hours to help a stranger move. Now, why would you do that?" Jared stroked his chin, pretending to be perplexed.

"Because I'm an idiot."

"No, because you like her, dumbass."

"I already told you I don't. I'm done dealing with situations where the girl is all in and I have to let her down."

"Well, it's a good thing you're not doing *anything* to give her the wrong impression."

"Shut up."

The most irritating part of this conversation was that he was right. I did like her. When I saw her struggling to juggle all of those boxes, the only thing I could think about was how adorably out of place she looked. And I didn't really want to help her move, but when I saw an easy opportunity to see her again, I snatched it up.

"Maybe you could stop letting girls down and start letting them in." Jared was still going on about this. "I get that your example of a relationship growing up was shit, but that doesn't mean you have to repeat that. You deserve someone great."

I handed him a few buckets of paint to bring in. "Can you get the rollers too?"

"Don't change the subject, man. I know you hate talking about serious shit, but I'm your best friend. Cut the BS and have a real conversation with me for once."

"I've got nothing to say."

The trunk of the van slammed shut, and I let Jared and me through the door in the back of the building.

"That's not true, but whatever, I'll drop it. Just because you've been bottling up every emotion you've ever had doesn't mean they aren't brimming to the surface, ready to spill over."

Once inside I took in the large, exposed ceilings and felt my excitement for this new endeavor wash over me. I tried to ignore Jared, but his outburst was picking at the back of my brain.

Even though I tried to deny it, I knew he was right. Having emotions was looked at as a weakness my entire childhood. My dad would always tell me to let everything wash off of me like a polished stone. A real man didn't feel sad, or scared, or worried, or even silly. One thing he didn't seem to have a problem with "real men" feeling was anger. That much he made very clear as he took out every toxic thought he ever had on my mom and me.

I looked over at Jared, who had already started opening the painting supplies. A feeling of pure gratefulness swept over me. I had never told him, but our friendship meant a lot to me. He had been there through all of my ups and downs, despite me never wanting to talk about it. When we were younger, I used to swing by his house on my bike, and we would ride for hours, not saying anything. Those moments saved me.

"This place is going to look amazing." Jared put his hands on his hips and looked around at the empty shell that would someday soon be bustling with people.

"All thanks to Eric and the investors," I mumbled.

Jared took a few steps toward me before lifting his hand and swiftly smacking me on the back of the head.

"Ow—hey. What the hell was that for?" I narrowed my eyes at him and rubbed the spot he had hit.

"Every successful business has financial backing. That doesn't mean shit without the vision. Luna, and this place, are all you. They wouldn't exist without your brain, so just shut up already about money and start bragging that you're about to own two of the most successful restaurants in the city."

I blew out the breath I had been holding and took in the place again. "You're right. I have come a long way, haven't I?"

"Damn right you have. Now start owning it."

I felt the corners of my mouth tugging up and nodded over at my best friend to signal a thank-you. He was right. This felt damn good, and I did need to start owning it.

Maybe it was time to take control of other aspects of my life too. My thoughts drifted to Al and my spontaneous offer to help her move tomorrow. Even though we had just met, there was something about her that I was undeniably drawn to. Sure, she was beautiful, but it was more than that. Maybe it was the fact that we would both rather be upstairs alone than at a party full of people. Maybe it was her slightly awkward demeanor and the way she didn't seem to be putting up any kind of front. Whatever it was, I found her easy to talk to. Since this was exceedingly rare for me, maybe I needed to stop questioning it and just see what happened.

THIRTEEN
AL

Pacing around my apartment, I triple-checked that I hadn't forgotten to pack up any loose items. The place was empty except for all of the boxes I'd staged in the bare living room. I glanced at my phone.

9:03.

I was nervous that Dean had forgotten about the arrangement we made yesterday. Although he definitely heard me say nine, he had never texted me to confirm. And without his number, I had no way of contacting him.

I shouldn't have canceled the U-Haul.

After another five minutes passed, my eyes started to burn and I could feel my throat constricting.

This is stupid. I will not cry.

I picked up my phone to see if a truck rental was still available when someone banged at my door.

My heart started beating out of my chest as I walked over to the entryway, checking my appearance in the hall mirror. I had on an oversized sweatshirt and leggings. My short hair was pulled up into a tiny ponytail, and the ends by my face had fallen loose. This morning's activity didn't lend well to a cute outfit, so this would have to do.

I pulled open the door to see Dean leaning against the frame. He was breathing hard, as if he had just gotten done sprinting a mile. He looked so cozy in gray sweatpants and a T-shirt. He smelled good too. I wondered what it would feel like to hug him.

"Sorry I'm late. I had to circle the block a few times to find a parking spot. Thankfully, one opened up across the street."

"I was about to give up on you."

He furrowed his brow. "It's, like, nine-oh-five. You had that little faith in me?"

I smirked. "Well, you do seem great and all, but you're essentially a stranger. I didn't even have your number to ask if you were still coming."

"So dramatic." He chuckled, and without hesitation, he pulled his phone out of his back pocket and started typing. Seconds later I heard my phone beep in the distance.

"Now you have my number. The next time I'm a few minutes late to help you move, please feel free to chew me out via text message."

I smiled. "Seriously, Dean, thank you so much for coming. It isn't every day that someone I barely know offers me free manual labor."

Stepping inside, I allowed him to walk past me.

"This it? You weren't kidding about this not taking long."

He walked around one of the piles of boxes and started playing with the tassel of an old lamp I had proudly thrifted.

"Are you sure your roommate is moving in with her boyfriend, or did you drive her away with your terrible taste in lamps?"

"Excuse you, that's an antique. It could be worth something."

"Is it?"

"I mean, probably not, but that's not the point. Eclectic interior design is in anyway. That lamp is cool."

He laughed. "Whatever you say, Al."

My heart fluttered when he said my name.

"This apartment is great." He took a few long strides to the kitchen and turned around, examining the older built-ins. "Bummer you have to move."

"It's fine. I've had a week to accept it. Besides, I could use the fresh start."

He tilted his head and gazed at me for a few seconds. "I know what you mean."

My palms were sweaty all of a sudden. Every time Dean looked at me, my stomach flipped. Getting through the next hour or so without saying something embarrassing was going to be a challenge.

It had been a while since I interacted with a man. Should I be flirtatious? I racked my brain trying to think of something witty to say. I was sick of being the girl that guys never took seriously. I wanted Dean, and I wanted to make that clear. Subtly, of course.

I started to walk to the kitchen to join Dean when my foot got caught on the rug I had rolled up on the floor. I let out a small gasp as I stumbled a few steps forward.

Dean was in front of me in an instant. He grabbed my elbows to steady me. "Whoa there."

Per usual, my cheeks immediately flushed bright red. "I'm such a klutz," I muttered, before attempting to take a step backward.

Dean kept a firm grip on my elbows. "Good thing you've got me to catch you." He was grinning ear to ear now.

"Thanks." I tried to come off as good-natured by smiling in

return, but my face contorted into something closer to a grimace. I cringed inwardly.

This was not off to a good start. How could I not have realized how awkward this would be when I agreed to it yesterday?

"So." Dean removed his hands from my elbows, and I felt cold at the loss of his touch. "Where is the new place?"

"Just over a few streets."

"I used to live with Jared for years. I thought living by myself would be a little boring, but having my own space is great. I could never go back."

I paused before answering. "Um. I'm actually moving in with roommates."

His eyebrows shot up. "Oh, my bad. I just assumed. Dumb of me. Are they friends from college?"

"Um, just friends," I replied, not wanting to admit to the guy I was crushing on that I was moving in with three strangers. "Should we get started?"

It dawned on me that Dean was also basically a stranger. Everyone that I was interacting with today was new in my life. Maybe I was branching out. *Take that, Jess and every other person that said I was terrible with new people.*

"Yes," he said, clapping his hands. "What should we bring down first? I'm thinking we should get the mattress over with."

We both walked to opposite ends of the full-sized bed covered in plastic and stared at it.

"Unless you want to tackle this yourself. What did you say yesterday? It's all about the technique?" He winked at me, and I rolled my eyes in response.

"I'm sure I could have done it."

Dean counted us down, and on "three" we both hoisted up our ends. Due to me being half his size, my end was much closer to the ground than his was.

We shuffled our way toward the door.

"Turn. Turn. Turn."

I started angling the mattress to the right, but Dean continued to shout commands at me.

"Turn where?" I shouted back.

Dean grunted before setting down his side. I followed suit.

He squeezed back through the doorframe before taking my side. He moved the mattress even more to the right so that it was almost parallel with the hallway outside and shoved it through with one swift push.

"Like that," he said, and flashed me a cocky grin.

I rolled my eyes. "Okay, hotshot. Your instructions were not clear, and sorry I'm not two hundred pounds of muscle."

"I thought you were going to do this yourself?" He grinned.

I tried not to notice his strong, tattooed biceps peeking out of his shirt. "I could have handled it."

At that, Dean threw his head back and laughed. "You're so stubborn."

We both picked up our ends again and maneuvered the mattress down the first flight of stairs.

When we got to the second-floor landing, Dean once again called out, "Turn. Turn more."

I lifted the mattress a little more and shoved it toward the wall.

"Not *that* way!" Dean shouted.

"Your instructions suck!" I yelled back. My forearms were killing me, and I had to set down my side again.

"Come on. It's obvious what I meant."

"Apparently not." I picked up the mattress and forced it the other way. It unwedged itself from the banister and scooted forward, toward Dean.

"There you go."

"It would have worked the other way too," I muttered.

"What was that?"

"Nothing," I called in a singsong voice.

It took us about ten minutes to wrestle the mattress down the rest of the stairs. I had to set it down two more times to find a better grip, and Dean continued to yell unclear instructions at me. When we finally got it across the street and gave it one last shove into Dean's van, he turned to me and offered his hand for a high five.

I crossed my arms and glared at him.

"What? We did it."

"I could have done without the yelling."

"Well, I could have done without you ignoring me."

I scowled. "Who made you in charge?"

Dean furrowed his brow before breaking into a laugh.

"What's so funny?"

"Just that we haven't even gone on a first date yet and we're already bickering about how best to move a piece of furniture." He ruffled my hair, and my irritation instantly dissolved.

I tried not to put too much thought into the words "first date" as we headed back upstairs. The rest of the items were small and considerably less heavy. The mattress was the only two-person job, so we got through the rest of the boxes without any more arguing.

"I can't believe we're almost done. I seriously owe you."

"Does this mean you're admitting I was right about the mattress?" He nudged my shoulder.

Was I imagining it or had he been looking for little ways to touch me all morning?

He looked down at my backpack, which was one of the few remaining items in the room. My laptop for work and a notebook were sitting out. Earlier that morning I had to reply to a few "emergency" emails after my boss texted me in a panic about some numbers Trent ran last week.

"Does this need to go down now?"

"That's just my work stuff. Let me put it away, and it should be ready to go." I grabbed everything from the floor and started stuffing it into the backpack.

"What do you do?"

"Um, I'm an analyst for this start-up downtown. I do mostly marketing, but also sales and revenue stuff too," I mumbled. I hated talking about work.

"So you're pretty smart, then," he stated as if he knew it for a fact.

"Apparently, I'm smart enough to be needed on a Saturday but not smart enough to deserve a promotion." I could tell I sounded bitter and needed to change the subject.

"That sounds pretty messed up."

"It's fine. It pays the bills, so..." I trailed off, picking up my bag from the floor and slinging it over my shoulder.

"You shouldn't settle though."

I scoffed. "Easy for you to say, Mr. Successful Restaurant Owner."

He tilted his head, studying me. "Nothing ever came easy for me."

The color drained from my face as I realized my blunder. "Of course not. I'm sorry." I hung my head, feeling ashamed at my tasteless comment. "I get it, you know? It wasn't easy for me either. That's kind of why I feel ridiculous for complaining about a job that pays me well."

He considered this. "I get that. But there's more to life than a paycheck. If it's making you miserable, it's not worth it."

We both stood there in an awkward silence before I moved toward the last of the items.

"Well, we're almost done." I hoped Dean would allow my change of subject.

He nodded before grabbing the few remaining items. I took one last look around to make sure we got everything, and stopped briefly to take in the empty apartment. It felt surreal to be doing this without Jess. I set the key on the countertop and locked the doorknob per my landlord's instructions and left my old home for the last time.

Downstairs, Dean climbed into the driver's seat of his van, and I joined him up front.

Desperate to break the weird tension between us, I turned to Dean. "Thanks again for helping me. You might have been right about the mattress."

His mouth turned up into an adorable half smile as he looked over at me. "Might have been?"

I sighed. "Okay, okay. You were right."

He chuckled. "Your conviction is cute."

A smile tugged at my lips. "Just keep going straight and turn right at the next stop sign."

Dean opened and closed his mouth. His eyebrows were drawn together, and it seemed like he was struggling to find something to say. Maybe my awkwardness was contagious. Normally, silence made me uncomfortable, but right now—with Dean—it wasn't so bad.

Minutes later we arrived in front of the Greystone. Staring up at my new home, I felt very hot despite the chilly morning temperatures. I was nervous to see my new roommates again. Why did I think living with strangers wasn't going to be totally and completely weird?

Nora sent me a message earlier this week that only she would be home right now. Cameron and Sean both had plans. At least it was less overwhelming this way. I took a deep breath and jumped out of the van.

Dean whistled next to me. "Wow, this place is sick."

"Al!" Nora exclaimed as she opened the front door. She rushed down the steps and threw up her arms as if to hug me but stopped abruptly a foot away. Normally, I would have been grateful that she remembered my aversion to being touched, but now the moment felt a little bit weird.

"Al," she repeated. "It's so nice to see you again. This is so exciting. How can I help?"

Dean shot me a puzzled expression that I pretended not to notice.

"Hey, Nora. Please don't feel like you have to help. We've got it under control. This is my—" I paused. "My friend" didn't feel appropriate to say, since we hardly knew each other. "This is Dean. He's helping me move. Dean, this is Nora."

Nora seemed to catch my hesitation and didn't ask for any clarification on our nonexistent relationship.

"Nice to meet you, Dean. And I insist on helping. How lazy would I be if I just watched you two trudge in boxes while I drank mimosas on the couch?"

"Well, Al and I got the mattress. We're pros at it now." Dean winked at me, and my stomach burst into butterflies.

We already had an inside joke.

Between the three of us, it only took thirty minutes to unload the van and get everything into my room. After we were done with the last box, Dean and I collapsed on the couch while Nora ran off to the kitchen. Seconds later she emerged with three glasses and a bottle of champagne.

She handed us both a glass and started pouring.

Dean mimed turning over his wrist and checking an imaginary watch. "It's not even eleven."

"But we're celebrating," Nora insisted.

"Just a small glass for me. I've got to get the van back. My friend has a gig tonight, and he'll be pissed if I don't get it back soon for him to pack up."

I froze mid-sip, remembering that it was Saturday. The day of the gig he never invited me to. Jared had mentioned it last night though. Would it be weird if I went?

"Ooh, your friend is in a band?" Nora asked.

"Yeah, they play mostly covers. They're playing in River North tonight." Dean looked right at me. "If you both are free, you should come."

Nora squealed. "That sounds perfect. I was going to suggest a night out in honor of Al moving in. Can our other roommates come?"

"Definitely. Mention the band and Jared's name and they'll waive the cover at the door."

The possibility of seeing Dean tonight was either making me excited or anxious, I couldn't tell. I didn't go out with new people often, and I was already feeling self-conscious about how I'd be perceived.

Nora and Dean spent a few more minutes making small talk while I nursed my champagne. I was never great at communicating in group settings, even if it was just the three of us. It always felt so hard to know when to interject, and I hated the idea of interrupting the flow of the conversation.

"All right," Dean said, setting down his empty glass. "This has been fun, but I've got to run. Hopefully I'll see you both tonight."

I stood up to walk him to the door. "Thanks again for the help with the move. I owe you dinner or something."

He gave me a lopsided smile and tipped his head, considering me. "What about lunch instead?"

"Sure, whatever. I seriously owe you."

"Okay, lunch it is. Let's go, I'm starving."

"Um, what? You mean now?"

"Yeah, let's go. I've got a little time to kill before I have to get the van back. Plus, I'm weak from the excessive manual labor you've exposed me to." He winked and gestured for me to follow him.

"Oh, but I should unpack."

I wasn't sure why I was trying to get out of more alone time with Dean. It was probably because if the two of us sat down to eat together, he was sure to notice something off about me and get the ick.

Dean leaned against the doorframe and cocked his head to the side, assessing me. He probably didn't get turned down often.

"C'mon. I'm starving. There's a diner right down the street. It'll be fast."

"Uh...okay. I guess we could do that." I started to follow him out the door before turning back. "Nora, do you want to come?"

She looked at me with bright eyes and a mischievous smile. "I'm good. I'll be here when you get back."

As I closed the door behind me, Dean chuckled. "Was that your attempt at giving us a chaperone?"

"Eh—no, of course not. I didn't want to be rude." My flustered tone was evident.

We made the short, awkward walk to the small diner just down the street. It was only awkward on my account. Dean was effortlessly making small talk about his new restaurant and the neighborhood while I just nodded and gave one-word responses.

Now, Dean was staring at me from across the booth. The most I had spoken was when I had placed my order just a few seconds ago. Just two scrambled eggs and toast because I was too nervous to enjoy anything substantial right now.

I felt stupid for being nervous, but in my defense, I hadn't gone out to a meal with a guy in *years*. Actually, maybe not ever, now that I was thinking about it.

"What are you thinking about?" Dean prodded gently.

"Um, just how this might be the first time I've gone out to eat with a guy," I answered honestly.

He frowned and drew his eyebrows together, displaying his confusion.

I regretted oversharing. "You probably think that's pathetic."

"Definitely not what I was thinking," he replied. "I'm just surprised. How could you have gone twenty-three years without sharing a meal with a man? It's impressive."

I snorted. "I mean, I've been out in groups obviously, but not so much one-on-one. I don't have too many guy friends that I'm close with, and dating has changed..." I let my words trail off, horrified that I brought up dating when this was a casual thank-you lunch.

Thankfully, Dean didn't look disgusted by my blunder and urged me to continue. "Please elaborate on that. How has dating changed? Are you saying people don't go out to dinner anymore?"

"I'm sure they do. I've just found dating to mostly consist of guys inviting me to their house at midnight."

He snorted. "Well, then I guess you've never dated."

"I guess I haven't." I folded my arms across my chest and looked down, suddenly feeling uncomfortable.

"Hey." Dean reached across the table and grabbed my arm. "I didn't mean to be a dick. What I should have said is that you, of all people, deserve to be taken out on a real date."

"Why me, 'of all people'?"

His green eyes twinkled, and he pulled his arm back. "I'm going to stop digging myself a hole right now."

I leaned my elbow on the table and rested my chin in my sweatshirt-covered hand to hide my smirk.

"So," he said, changing the subject, "did I hear Nora say that it was 'nice to see you again'? I thought she was a friend."

I inhaled deeply before sighing, knowing I had been

caught. "I found the house through a roommate-wanted ad," I confessed. "I don't really know any of them."

Dean's smile dropped immediately, and his eyebrows drew together. "Is that safe?"

I laughed, secretly delighted that he sounded concerned for my well-being. "You saw Nora. I'm no expert, but she's not exactly the criminal-mastermind type."

Dean didn't look convinced. "For all you know, she has this whole scheme where she steals the identity of unsuspecting roommates and sells them on the black market."

"You're ridiculous."

"Hey." He threw his hands up, and his face finally broke out into a smile. "I'm just looking out for you, kid."

I rolled my eyes. "Kid? Really?"

"Once you hit thirty, everyone in their twenties seems like a kid."

"Geez, you are old."

"Stop that," he said, while playfully nudging my knee with his underneath the table.

My stomach felt warm and fluttery.

"So, no judgment, but *why* did you decide to live with complete strangers?"

"Honestly?" I snuck a glance at Dean before returning my gaze to my lap. "I just wanted to step outside of my comfort zone for once. I didn't have many friends growing up, and then ever since I met Jess in college, we've been attached at the hip. I've never had to challenge myself or make my own friends."

"I get that." He nodded. "Jared was pretty much my only friend growing up."

"You seem like you have a lot of friends now."

He shook his head. "Looks can be deceiving. Sure, I have a lot of acquaintances but not a lot of people who really know me."

"I feel like no one really knows me."

"Why is that?"

I started fidgeting with my sweatshirt sleeve. Crap, his empathetic eyes were making me overshare again.

"I went to this snobby private school. No one was mean to me or anything, but I never really fit in," I muttered, trying and failing to hide my discomfort. "And my mom—she's amazing... it's just that it's always been hard to talk to her. I was struggling at the school that she worked so hard to get me into. I didn't want to seem ungrateful. Anyway, long story short, I was always self-conscious, and that just amplified it. Now, it's hard for me to just open up and meet new people without being constantly concerned that they secretly don't like me or something."

"That's tough." Dean sat back in the booth, crossing his arms. "I get it, you know. More than you probably think. I always thought my mom was hard to talk to too. But after she passed away, I wished I had tried harder."

"Shit, I'm sorry about your mom. Here I am going on and on while you have real problems."

"You have real problems too." He hesitated before continuing. "What about your dad?"

"He's not in the picture. He bailed when I was pretty young." I was surprised at how easy it was to open up to him.

"Crappy dads," Dean said while not meeting my eyes. "Another thing I can relate to."

The food arrived just in time to ease the tension of the heavy conversation.

We spent the rest of the meal chatting about our lives and lighter topics. He told me more about how he opened his first restaurant. I told him all about my job that I despised and how I craved something more. When the check arrived, I was shocked at how fast the time had gone by. Connecting with people wasn't my strong suit, especially when I was insanely attracted to them.

I reached for my wallet, but before I could grab it, Dean pulled out cash and handed it to our server.

"Hey, I'm supposed to pay. This is a 'thank you for helping me move' lunch, remember?" I tried to flag the waitress to come back.

Dean smiled and winked at me. "Shoot, I completely forgot. I guess we'll just have to do this again."

FOURTEEN
DEAN

The rain splattered against the windows of Luna and distorted the view outside. Staring out into the street, I let my mind drift off. Seeing Al today had left me more confused than ever. It should be easy to write her off, but it was hard to ignore how effortlessly the conversation flowed with her. Hell, I had already told her things about myself that I'd only ever talked to Jared about. I needed to nip this in the bud before anything got complicated.

Would it be so bad to let someone in?

Shaking my head, I purged my mind of the intrusive thought.

Sighing deeply, I turned back around to survey the restaurant. About half of the tables were full of people enjoying their food and talking exuberantly. There was a lull right now, but we were booked solid with reservations for later tonight. Thankfully, we had a large, dedicated staff that was more than capable of handling everything while some of us took the night off.

Bells chimed at the front of the restaurant. Eric and Tiff

walked in and scanned the crowd before seeing me at the bar. Tiff made a beeline for the seat next to me while Eric went around to a table of six guests, ready to schmooze, I'm sure. Chatting up patrons was never my strong suit, but Eric could talk to a brick wall if he had to.

Tiff reached me and planted a kiss on my cheek before sitting down and ordering a drink.

"I'm so excited to see Jared play," she gushed.

"Eh, he's all right. Whatever you do, don't compliment him too much, or it'll go straight to his head."

Tiff giggled. "What have you been up to today?"

Feeling guilty, I froze. I needed to play this as nonchalantly as possible. "Funny thing, I actually ran into your friend Al last night. She needed help moving to a new apartment, so I offered to bring over my van."

Tiff glared at me.

"Don't look at me like that." I stared down into my glass of whiskey. "She's a cool girl. Maybe we could be friends."

"Right, because you have so many female friends." She sighed, exasperated. "You're both adults and can do whatever you want. I just feel like she's going to be taken with you when you pull her in and then be heartbroken when you're over it. She's a sweet girl. I just wish she'd meet some more genuine people."

"You don't think her friends are genuine?" I asked, sipping my drink to hide my interest.

She shrugged. "I like Jess. She invites me to hang out all the time, and she can be a lot of fun. I just think she doesn't always have Al's best interests in mind. Like, for instance, one time during their freshman year, Jess dragged Al to a frat party even though she didn't want to go. Then, at two a.m., I get a call from Al begging me for a ride because Jess ditched her for some guy and every cab company was booked. When I picked her up, she kept thanking me over and over again and making excuses for Jess. I didn't care what she had to say. It's BS to leave your girlfriend alone at a party. Anything could happen."

My grip tightened on my glass. "Sounds like a shitty friend."

"Don't go telling Al that I told you that story. She'd be pissed if I soured you toward Jess." She gave me a stern look. "Now why are you so insistent on corrupting another one of my friends anyway?"

"She's easy to talk to," I admitted.

Tiff's face softened at that, and she reached out to squeeze my forearm.

"Sorry to interrupt, is this seat taken?" Sarah, wearing a very tight pink dress, slid onto the other stool next to mine without waiting for an answer.

Tiff gave her a polite smile. "Are you going to Jared's show tonight too?"

Sarah leaned into me so that her breasts were grazing my arm. "Uh-huh. Dean invited me."

Shit, I forgot about that.

"Did he now?"

I didn't have to look to know that Tiff was shooting me a dirty look.

"Well, most of the staff is coming," I said, trying to brush off Sarah's comment.

I downed the remaining contents of my glass. It was going to be a long night.

"You all ready to go? Figured we could get there early and grab one of those booths near the front." Eric came up behind Tiff and me and clasped a hand on each of our shoulders.

"Let's get out of here," I said, grateful for the escape.

FIFTEEN
AL

Peeking out from the bathroom door, I glanced from side to side. I had just taken a shower and had stupidly forgotten to bring a change of clothes. Living with strangers, especially of the male variety, was going to take some getting used to.

The coast was clear.

Gripping my towel tighter, I made a dash toward my door. At the exact moment I entered the hallway, Sean exited his room, bumping into me. My death grip on my towel thankfully left me unexposed.

"Oh, Al—um...I'm sorry." Sean's face turned beet red.

If I had a mirror, I'm sure mine wouldn't look that different. "It's fine," I mumbled.

Before I could move past him, Cameron came barreling up the stairs.

"Impromptu toga party?" he asked.

"Um, no, I'm just trying to get to my room."

"Oh, sorry." While I stepped left to move around Sean, he stepped to his right to get out of my way, which caused us to bump into each other again.

Privacy, my ass.

"So what's the vibe tonight? I'm trying to decide what to wear." Cameron, completely oblivious to my discomfort, leaned against the wall and waited expectantly for my answer.

I crossed both of my arms over my chest. "Um, I don't know. Casual?"

"Are we discussing outfit options?" Nora poked her head out from behind the door to her room. "What are you wearing?" she asked me.

"This, apparently," I mumbled at the same time Cam said, "It's *casual*."

Nora rolled her eyes. "Stop being snobby, Cam. You know you're just going to wear the same thing you always do."

Cam brought his hand to his heart. "I'm offended."

"Um, I'm going downstairs," Sean announced, before extracting himself from me and our awkward run-ins.

Nora took his spot and grabbed my arm. "Come on, let's look at your options."

"Show me when you've narrowed them down," called Cam.

Apparently, changing in peace was not an option in this house.

"You look great. You need to wear that," Nora encouraged.

"I feel like I'm going to a club or something."

At Nora's insistence, I tried on one of the few dresses in my closet. It was a simple, short black number with spaghetti straps. It wasn't too short, but it did fall quite a bit above my knees. A far cry from my usual jeans and a T-shirt. I only owned this dress in the first place because Jess had given it to me as a gift.

"Stop, you're wearing that."

"Fine, but I'm wearing my boots."

Sifting through the boxes of clothes on my closet floor, I pulled out my trusted combat boots. I also grabbed an oversized bomber jacket to throw on top.

"So, what's the deal with you and Dean anyway?" Nora sat back on my bed, trying to sound casual.

Wow, we were getting into the girl talk already.

"He's a friend of a friend. I barely know him, but we ran into each other last night, and he wasn't doing anything, so he offered to help me."

"Uh-huh. I'm not buying that. Nobody just offers to help someone they don't know move out of the kindness of their heart. I think he's into you."

I snorted. "I wish. He's way out of my league."

"You're dreaming, Al. You're literally gorgeous. I'm telling you he definitely has at least a mini crush on you."

"And I'm telling you he was just being nice. He hasn't even flirted with me or anything."

Thinking back to the restaurant, I knew that wasn't completely true, but I didn't want to get my hopes up that anything could happen between us.

"I guess we'll find out tonight at the show."

I paused mid-mascara application. "What do you mean by that?"

"Well, it should be obvious whether or not he invited you as a date. If he goes out of his way to spend time with you at his friend's gig, then he must like you. If he just says hi and goes about his night, then maybe you're right and I've completely misread the situation."

"I'm telling you it's not a date."

"Are you both almost ready?" we heard Sean call from the kitchen.

"We'll be right down," we both hollered back.

Nora rushed back into her room to grab her purse. I sat on my bed to pull on my boots, taking in my surroundings. My new bedroom was well on its way to being set up. My bed was made, and I had hung a few photographs and placed my rug and my "ugly" lamp. It felt surreal to be calling somewhere else home, but I felt excited about it.

The bathroom situation, not so much.

In the kitchen, everyone was already making themselves a drink.

"Let me guess, vodka soda?" Cameron asked, lifting a glass.

"It's easiest on the hangover," I replied, making a mental note not to drink too much tonight. I tended to overdo it without thinking when I needed to ease my nerves, and I wanted to make a good first impression. One that did not include clutching a toilet later tonight.

"Cheers to Al's first night in the house."

We all knocked glasses and started sipping our drinks while music played from a Bluetooth speaker someone had set up.

"What kind of show is this?" asked Sean.

"I'm not sure. I think Dean said they're a cover band."

"And someone in the band is friends with your boyfriend?"

Nora elbowed Cameron in the ribs.

"Ow. What was that for?"

I blushed. "No, no, no. I hardly know Dean. He's just a friend of a friend."

The three of them exchanged glances.

"What?" I demanded.

"I don't want to overstep, since we just met," Cam started. "But he helped you move *and* invited you to his friend's show. I think he might be into you."

"That's what I said," Nora exclaimed her agreement.

I looked down at my drink, already regretting my resolution

not to overdo it. How was I going to get through this night relatively sober?

"I suck at flirting with guys," I blurted out.

Sean sipped his drink and avoided eye contact while Cameron and Nora studied me.

"Why do you think that?"

"I don't know. I'm just not that talkative. And even when I am talking to a guy, I don't have the whole 'bat my eyelashes and make myself irresistible' thing. They always just see me as a friend or not even that."

"When was the last time you went on a date?" Nora asked.

I pursed my lips, not wanting to admit the answer. "I mean, I've hung out with guys before. Like, you know, the whole 'go over to each other's apartments and *watch movies*.'" I made an air-quotes gesture. "Or meet up at a bar. But I don't know if I've ever been on an official date."

"You've never had a boyfriend?" Cameron looked shocked.

I shook my head.

"Hey, lay off," Sean interjected. "Stop with the third degree."

"No, it's okay. I know I can be a little bit of a pushover when it comes to this stuff. My friend Jess tells me I never communicate what I want or how I'm feeling."

Nora walked around the kitchen island and put a hand on my arm. "Well, how do you feel about this guy?"

I sighed. "I mean, I guess I like him. He's easy to talk to. But there's no way he's into me. He's older and successf—"

"Stop that right now," Cam interrupted me. "There will be no self-deprecation in this house."

Nora patted my shoulder. "All you have to do is talk to him. Don't overthink it."

I forced a smile. "Seriously, can we stop talking about me? What about you all? Are any of you in a relationship?"

"I for one have been enjoying dating around. I was with my ex-boyfriend for two years, and it feels so good to only worry about myself," Cameron said.

"Single as a pringle."

Sean snuck an expectant glance at Nora as she said that before muttering, "I'm not seeing anyone either."

I wondered if anything was going on there.

An hour later we arrived at the venue. The lights were dim, and people were crowded around a large bar in the center of the room. The stage was in the back, and it looked like the band was about to start playing. Sean and Cameron split off from us to get drinks for the group. Nora and I hung back away from the bar, where there was more space.

"You should text Dean that you're here."

"I'm sure we'll run into him. I don't want to seem desperate." Secretly, I just wanted more time to mentally prepare myself before seeing him.

"Fine, fine. Do you want to run to the bathroom with me? I want to go before there's a line."

"I'm good. I'll wait here for the guys."

Nora weaved her way through the crowd. Feeling awkward waiting by myself, I pulled out my phone to check the time.

I felt a rush of excitement as I saw a new message.

> Dean: Let me know when you get here. We're at a table near the stage.

I put my phone away, deciding to wait until my group was reunited before responding.

"Ouch, are you blowing off my text?"

Surprised, I looked up to see Dean in front of me. He had

one hand in his pocket and the other was holding a beer. He looked effortlessly cool in a light-gray faded graphic T-shirt and black jeans. His hair was hanging in his face. I resisted the urge to reach up and tuck it behind his ear.

What was *wrong* with me?

"Hey, oh. No. Sorry, I was waiting for my friends. They're getting drinks. They should be back any minute."

"No worries, I'm just messing with you. I'll wait with you."

"So," I hesitated, willing myself to be smooth. "Seems like a good crowd."

"Yeah, they've been pulling a decent amount of people lately."

"I'm excited to hear them play," I said, feeling lame.

"Did you get settled into your new room yet? I hope you found a place for your priceless antique lamp."

I lightly shoved his chest. "I did, thank you very much. And the rest of it is coming along. I've got my bed set up, which is the most important thing."

"Oh, the bed is *definitely* the most important thing," Dean replied, wiggling his eyebrows.

My cheeks flushed. "Oh my God, I meant to sleep. The bed is important so I have somewhere to sleep." I paused, all of a sudden concerned about coming off too innocent. "I mean, not that the other stuff you do on a bed isn't great too." My cheeks reddened deeper.

His eyes crinkled as he started to laugh. "Oh really, tell me more."

By some miracle, Sean and Cameron chose that moment to reappear with drinks, interrupting our conversation.

"Sorry, that line took forever." Cameron handed me a vodka soda that I eagerly accepted.

Sean scanned the crowd for Nora.

"She went to the bathroom. She should be back soon," I answered his unspoken question.

He nodded and took a sip of one of the drinks he was holding.

"Dean, these are my other roommates, Sean and Cameron." I gestured to the two guys as I said their names. "Sean. Cameron. This is Dean."

Dean scrunched his brow and dropped his smile, and I wondered if he thought it was weird that I lived with two guys. He seemed to brush off his confused expression and replaced his frown with a charming smile. He threw out his hand to Cameron and then to Sean.

"Hey, good to meet you. Thanks for coming. The band loves it when these places are as packed as possible."

"Well, I think they'll love tonight given the crowd surrounding the bar," Sean replied.

Nora appeared behind Cameron, wrapping her arms around his neck. "Let's go get a better spot by the stage." She took the drink from Sean's outstretched hand. "Dean, hi. I didn't even see you lurking there."

"We've got a table up front. You can put your stuff down there."

As we weaved our way through the crowd, Dean put his hand on the small of my back and leaned in so that his mouth was close to my ear. "You live with two guys, huh?"

I was too shocked by his touch to respond, so instead I froze and stared straight ahead like an idiot. Dean winked at me and then broke off as we arrived at the table. Eric and Tiff were there as well.

"Al, hi," Tiff squealed, embracing me.

I introduced her and Eric to my roommates. Everyone was drinking and making small talk when Tiff pulled me aside.

"Dean told me that you were coming. I'm so happy to see you."

"It's great to see you too."

"How's the new place? Jess mentioned at happy hour that you were moving in with some people you met online."

My eyes burned at the mention of them hanging out without me again. I understood that they were friends, but I wished they would think to invite me sometimes.

"It's great. They seem nice so far."

Tiff beamed at me. "That's amazing. I'm so proud of you for branching out."

I took a sip of my drink, feeling self-conscious at her praise. "I was nervous at first, but I think I'm glad I did it."

"I'm so happy for you." She squeezed my arm. "So, you and Dean, huh?"

"No, it's not like that at all. He invited me to be nice. Plus, he mentioned that a crowd is good for the band, so..."

"Seriously, just be careful. I know he's nice and charming, but he is not boyfriend material. That guy is the most commitment-phobic person I've ever met."

I scoffed. "Who said I was looking for a boyfriend? I swear you and Jess act like I'm looking for a husband to deflower me or something. I'm allowed to just hang out or even casually date if I want to."

"Of course, of course," she said hurriedly. "I know that. I'm sorry, I'm not trying to upset you." She paused, clearly considering what to say next. "I just want you to find someone who's nice to you. Not the kind of guy that blows you off after a few dates."

I folded my arms over my chest, considering this. "And Dean is that kind of guy?" I asked, trying my best to sound like I didn't care.

"The guy brings a new date around almost every time I see

him. They always seem so interested and engaged in him, and he barely registers them. Even now, he invited a girl who works at the restaurant"—she gestured to a pretty redhead smiling at Dean—"but he's hardly giving her the time of day."

Just then, Eric came over and started to pull Tiff toward the dance floor as the band walked onstage.

"Hey, Al." He nodded in my direction. "Come on, babe, let's get a spot up front."

I smiled at them as they walked off, hand in hand.

As casually as possible, I snuck a look back at Dean and the mystery girl sitting next to him. My own nerves had caused me to miss her the first time we approached the table, but now I couldn't look away. She looked drop-dead gorgeous wearing a dress that I could only fantasize about pulling off.

Feeling queasy, I took a huge sip of my drink. How could I be so stupid thinking Dean might want to talk to me tonight? I let everyone get in my head, telling me that he must have a crush on me. Clearly, they were wrong, because no guy that could pull a girl like that would be interested in me.

Dean broke his gaze from the redhead and glanced over at me. I quickly looked away and grabbed Nora.

"Do you see that girl he's with?" I whispered.

She glanced at them.

"Don't look," I hissed.

"How am I supposed to see her?"

"Are we talking about the leggy redhead?" Cam whispered, his head appearing between us.

I nodded. "But be discreet."

At that moment we all snuck a glance, only to be met with Dean's green eyes staring right back at us.

"*Shit*, he totally saw us."

"What are you talking about?" Sean joined our pack, and his voice was far too loud.

The three of us shushed him simultaneously.

Before we could fill him in, the girl brushed by us with Dean in tow. She was pulling him by his T-shirt, and he was allowing her to drag him onto the dance floor. My cheeks burned.

"I'm so stupid."

"No, you aren't," Nora insisted at the same time Cam told me to "Knock it off."

"You win some, you lose some." He coaxed my glass closer to my lips. "Now come on. Drink up and let's have some fun."

SIXTEEN
DEAN

"Stop being so stiff," Sarah whined. She tugged at my hand and placed it on her stomach.

I tried to go along with her movements, but my body seemed vehemently against it. Had I imagined it or did Al look a little crushed when she saw Sarah?

It was a good thing, her seeing me with another girl. That would definitely get the right message across.

Even as the thought crossed my mind, and as Sarah was shaking her ass into my crotch, I found myself searching the crowd for Al. It made me irrationally irritated that she had shown up with two guys. The unfamiliar feeling of jealousy was likely the reason I was allowing Sarah to be all over me now.

I spotted Al toward the edge of the dance floor. Her short frame was getting absorbed by the crowd. The taller guy she had introduced me to—Sean?—was hovering near her and Nora, ensuring they weren't bumped into. His kind gesture toward her made me feel instantly possessive. I flexed my hands to keep them from balling into a fist.

Get it together.

I was being ridiculous. Sean seemed to be staring at Nora, and I swear I saw Cam leaning into the male bartender earlier. They were harmless. And even if they *were* interested in Al, that was also not my problem, I reminded myself.

Al and Nora were bopping along to the music. Al looked relaxed for once and like she was genuinely having fun. She looked up at me as if sensing my gaze. We locked eyes for a few seconds before I felt a hand stroking my upper arm. Al ripped her eyes away from mine just as I tore my arm away from Sarah, trying to hide my distaste.

"What's the matter with you?" she said, frustrated I wasn't being my usual flirtatious self.

"Need a drink," I mumbled.

I tore through the crowd without waiting to see if she followed me. Normally, I would be all in for someone like Sarah. Now all I was thinking about was how Al was perceiving me. When I made it back to the table, Sarah shoved past me, clearly wanting me to know that she was fed up with my behavior.

"Damn, what did you say to piss her off?" Eric asked as he joined me in the booth, his forehead glistening from dancing.

"Nothing. She's just mad I'm not all over her."

"Why the hell not? She already knows you won't commit, might as well have some fun." He elbowed me in the ribs, but I scowled in response.

"I'm not interested."

He chuckled. "And that wouldn't have anything to do with a cute brunette that happens to be here tonight, right?"

Ignoring him, I resumed openly staring at Al as she lost all of her inhibitions, singing along to the covers. Her legs looked amazing in that tiny black dress. I shifted, feeling my pants tightening as I watched her move to the music.

I wanted her, and I was sick of fighting it. She was having an effect on me, and I was becoming more and more determined to do something about it.

SEVENTEEN
AL

Nora and I collapsed at the table, completely out of breath. We had sung our hearts out to every song we knew and jumped around so much that I knew my legs would be sore in the morning. I was buzzing from the music and the several drinks we had downed. Seeing Dean with that girl had made me feel like such an idiot. As a result, I might have had more to drink than I was planning.

"Hey, how are you two feeling? Please drink this." Sean had appeared by Nora's side, looking concerned. He handed her a glass of water.

"Sean!" she screamed, flinging her arms around his neck. "You're so sweet, thank you."

She chugged the water before resting her head on the table.

On the dance floor, it was painfully obvious that Sean was trying to get Nora's attention. While Nora hadn't blown him off, it did seem like she was pretending to be oblivious. Like, one time he had grabbed her hand, and she immediately grabbed Cam's and turned it into a clunky group dance.

"Shit, how much did she have to drink?" Sean's eyebrows pulled together above his glasses.

Feigning innocence, I shrugged. I felt a little guilty that I had been slinging back tequila with her fifteen minutes earlier.

"One thing about Nora is that she loves to have fun but rarely drinks. She can overdo it sometimes," he whispered.

She popped her head up. "I resent that. I'm perfectly fine."

Sean chuckled. "Okay, tiger. Whatever you say."

She stretched her arms upward and yawned. "I am pretty beat though. I think I'm going to get a cab."

I glanced at my phone. "But it's only eleven thirty."

"Sorry, Al."

She got up unsteadily, and I started to push myself off the table when Sean stopped me. "Hey, you should stay. I'm not much of a partier either. I can make sure Nora gets home okay."

Nora winked at me from behind Sean's back. Something was *definitely* going on there.

"Um, okay, are you sure? I don't have to stay."

"No, please stay," Nora responded. "You can wait for Cam. He's been flirting with that bartender all night."

"Okay." I still felt unsure.

With Nora leaving, Dean on a date, Eric and Tiff making out in the booth, and Cam trying to pick up some guy, staying here felt pretty unappealing. But, at the same time, if something was going on with Nora and Sean, I didn't want to impose on them either.

"Get home safe, you two." I forced a smile.

I'd wait here a little longer, sober up, and call a cab for myself.

After they left, I tried not to feel sorry for myself, but a pressure was building behind my eyes. I thought all of these new friendships were falling into place, yet I was still alone at a bar on a Saturday night.

"Screw it." I knocked back the remainder of the drink I was still holding.

I was about to get up to leave when Dean walked over from the bar and straddled the seat next to me.

"It looked like you were having fun out there."

My cheeks burned at the thought of him seeing my embarrassing dance moves.

"Yeah, the band is really good."

He was sitting so close to me that his knee bumped my bare leg as he readjusted in the chair. I hated that I felt butterflies at the mere brush of his leg.

"I kept trying to track you down in that crowd, but you and Nora were all over the place." He grinned, nudging my arm with his elbow.

"Oh, yeah. I guess."

He frowned at my short response and looked down at his shoes.

"Um, are you having fun? I haven't seen your date in a while." I could have kicked myself for bringing that up, but I wasn't great with subtleties after drinking.

His eyebrows shot up. "You mean Sarah? She just works at Luna. It wasn't a date."

"You two looked pretty cozy on the dance floor." I forced a smile and tried to pretend like we were friends. "Maybe you should go for it. You'd be, like, the most attractive couple ever."

He scowled. "We weren't that cozy."

"That's not what it looked like from over here," I muttered, bitterness creeping into my tone.

Why bother putting on a front of the cool, chill girl? It was doubtful I'd see Dean again after tonight, except maybe in passing.

He dipped his head to my level and tried to meet my eyes. "Are you...jealous?"

"Me? What? No, definitely not. Just making an observation." I flushed. "Why would I be jealous? We barely know each other."

"I'm trying to remedy that."

"Remedy what?"

"The fact that we barely know each other." He started drumming on the table. He seemed to be fidgeting a lot. "Why did you think I asked you to come tonight?"

I hesitated, feeling his eyes on me. "Technically, Jared asked me to come tonight," I retorted.

"You're going to get me on a technicality, huh?" he asked, grinning. "Well, I wanted to see you, for what it's worth."

A small snort escaped me. "Okay, sure."

"What?" he demanded.

"No offense, but that sounds like a line. A bullshit line."

"It's not a line," he insisted.

"Okay, then what? You want to be friends or something?"

"Not particularly."

I glared at him, my eyebrows furrowing. "I don't know what you're trying to tell me."

He laughed and shook his head. "I don't know either. All I do know is that I can't seem to stay away from you."

My heart was beating so fast I was sure he could hear it. He scooted his chair even closer to me, so that his knees were fully pressed into the side of my leg.

"And for the record, lifting heavy boxes is not a passion of mine." He smirked and looked down. "If I'm being honest, I hate moving so much that I hired someone the last time I had to do it."

"Then *why* did you offer?"

"You're really going to make me spell it out?" He threw his

head back and softly rolled his eyes, all with a smirk on his face. "I offered so that I could see you again." He sat back and ran his hand through his hair. "I may have thought about you a few times since Eric's party."

My eyes narrowed. "Then why didn't you text me?" I challenged. "We wouldn't even be talking right now if we hadn't run into each other yesterday."

"Look, I admit I don't have an amazing track record with women. I thought you were cute, but I felt bad making a move after Tiff begged me not to." He looked away from me sheepishly. "I kind of felt like I owed her after hooking up with a few of her friends already. Plus, you seemed nice. I didn't want to subject you to me."

"I'm an adult, you know? I can choose what and what not to subject myself to."

Dean leaned forward, forcing his eyes into my line of vision. "I was hoping you'd say that because it's becoming increasingly hard to stop thinking about you."

I crossed my arms. "For the record, parading another girl in front of me isn't usually a turn-on for me."

Sighing, he stood up and grabbed my hand. "Can we *please* forget that ever happened? I was trying to prove a point to myself, and I failed miserably."

I wasn't completely sure what he meant, but he seemed sincere, so I nodded.

He tugged my hand. "Come on, the band is about to start again."

I hesitated before following him to the open floor by the stage, already littered with people waiting. Even with the drinks in my system, I was a ball of nerves at our close proximity.

The four band members took the stage. Jared caught sight of Dean and stuck his tongue out and winked. Dean chuckled and grabbed onto my waist like it wasn't the first time he had held me close. *Whoa.* Subtly, I tried to take deep breaths through my nose to lower my pulse.

"You all look beautiful tonight!" Jared yelled into the mic. The crowd screamed their approval. "Thanks for coming. Here's another throwback."

The band launched into an upbeat '90s song that I loved. My inhibitions were lowered, and my body immediately took over. I started to jump around, not even caring if Dean thought I looked stupid. When I remembered to look over, he was bobbing right alongside me. He looked down and smiled.

We danced like that for a few more songs. He even twirled me at one point. My smile was huge and permanently plastered to my face. Did he actually *like* me? It didn't feel real, but he sure seemed to be giving all the signs.

I guess our conversation earlier hadn't exactly been a declaration of his feelings for me...but it was pretty close, right? I mean, he said he couldn't stay away from me. That had to mean he liked me.

The last song wound down, and the rest of the band left the stage, leaving only Jared front and center with his guitar. "All right, folks. This is our last song for the night, and I'm going to slow it down."

He launched into a soft, melodic song, and the crowd began to sway.

Big hands grabbed my hips, and a hard torso pressed lightly against my back. Surprised, I suddenly went rigid.

"Is this okay?" Dean's deep voice whispered in my ear, his hot breath sending tingles down my neck.

I nodded, the back of my head rubbing against his chest, and resumed swaying to the song. One of his hands inched up to my stomach, and I felt a warmth growing inside me with each brush of my back against his body. I felt a strong urge to turn around so the front of our bodies could press into each other. Instead, I leaned even more into Dean, increasing the friction between us.

"You're beautiful, you know that?" he breathed into my ear again.

"Mmm." I sighed, turning my head to look up at him.

At that moment, the music faded away. Without the magic of the dim lights and soft background song, I felt embarrassed at how all over Dean I was. I went to pull away from him, but he held on and pressed a kiss to the back of my head. He moved from behind me and slid his arm around my waist, guiding me back to the table.

It was then that I noticed the redhead from earlier. She was leaning against the table glaring at me.

Yikes.

When we got closer, she moved her attention to Dean and pursed her full lips. She put a hand on his shoulder and did her best to pretend he didn't still have his arm around me.

"Hey there, I was looking for you. Do you want to get out of here?"

He glanced down at me before returning his gaze to her. "I'm going to stick around a little longer. Get home safe, okay?"

She didn't bother hiding her disappointment as she snatched up her purse from the table. Before stalking off, she leaned down toward me. "Be careful with him. He's an asshole."

Her words felt like a bucket of ice-cold water. Everything about what he did tonight played into the narrative Tiff had warned me about.

All of a sudden, I had a thought. Was he trying to get me to go home with him? Was he hoping we'd leave together? Did he want to have *sex*? My body might have been ready for that, but my brain was screaming at me to take heed of all the warnings.

My mind went into overdrive as I tried not to let my panic show on the outside.

While I wasn't a virgin, I was also not terribly experienced. Going home and sleeping with a guy I barely knew was not something I had ever done. Racking my brain, I tried to remember what underwear I was wearing. Probably nothing cute.

Dean turned to look down at me. His face was only inches from mine when I looked up.

Shit. Shit. Shit.

"So...do you—"

Before I could go into full-blown panic mode, Cameron ambled up to us and threw his hands in the air exasperatedly.

"Men suck. I was flirting with that bartender all night and then just now he tells me he *lives* with his boyfriend. What a waste of my time."

Dean didn't step away from me, but Cameron seemed to be completely oblivious to the palpable sexual tension radiating between us.

"I'm over this. Do you want to go get food?"

I didn't even look at Dean's reaction before nodding my head.

"Yes, let's go. I'm starving."

Cameron spun around on his foot and sauntered toward the exit, signaling me to follow.

"Sorry, that's my cue," I said, backing away from Dean and toward the exit.

"Al, wai—"

"Thanks again for the invite," I spat the words out of my mouth, not giving him the chance to speak. "Text me!" I exclaimed before I darted for the door.

"Oh my God," Cameron moaned as he stuffed the last bite of his burrito into his mouth. "This is better than sex."

The fluorescent lights and the sticky booths of the late-night dive we were at had the reality of tonight setting in for me.

"I'm not so sure about that." I stared down at my half-eaten burrito.

"What's got you all down and out?"

"I think I messed up."

"Please elaborate."

I exhaled before blurting it all out. "I'm pretty sure Dean was flirting with me, and I think he might have almost asked me to go home with him, but being the awkward human that I am, I shut him down before he could even ask and raced out of the bar like it was on fire."

Cameron's eyes went wide. "Oh my God. I'm such an idiot. I saw you talking to him, but I wasn't even paying attention to the vibe. I was too annoyed about the stupid bartender." He reached across the table, grabbing my arm. "I am *so* sorry. I cockblocked you, didn't I? I completely interrupted whatever you two were talking about."

"No, no, no. It's okay. I was the only cockblock responsible for my misfortune. When I realized what he might ask, I couldn't get out of there fast enough. I didn't even let him get a word in." I put my forehead in my hands and groaned. "I'm so dumb—that was probably my only shot."

"I doubt that was your only shot. If anything, you kept him interested. He's probably not used to girls running out on him." Cameron shrugged and reached over to grab the remainder of my food. "Why were you so freaked out at the idea of him asking to leave together, anyway?"

I picked at my cuticles, feeling a little uncomfortable. "I've only slept with a few guys before, and I knew each of them at least a little bit. I just met Dean, and from what I've heard, he seems to have *a lot* more experience than me."

"Don't even worry about that. He won't care how many people you've slept with. The only question is, do you *want* to sleep with him?"

I nodded and hung my head. "Ugh. I think I do. It's so frustrating. I never get caught up in a guy like this."

"Then text him. I bet he's still awake."

"It's not that simple. I'm not sure I *only* want to sleep with him. I don't think I could handle him not wanting anything to do with me afterward, which, according to everyone, is his style. I mean, you saw it—even tonight, when he was hitting on me, he had another girl with him."

"Hmm, that is tough." He gave me a sympathetic look. "I say just wait and see what happens. You just started hanging out. Best case scenario, you fall madly in love; worse case, he might break your heart a little, and you'll get over it eventually. That's what our twenties are for anyway. You can't stress about making mistakes until you're thirty."

I snorted. "Please tell that to my brain. I'm constantly worried about making mistakes."

Cam rolled his eyes. "Please, I could write a five-hundred-page novel filled with mistakes. And that's just from when I was twenty-two."

Laughing, I snatched the last bite of my burrito back from Cam's clutches.

"Can I be frank with you?" Cam asked.

"Might as well."

"Maybe he does get around a lot. But in my experience, those guys are usually the best in bed."

I giggled and threw my napkin in his direction, trying not to regret my decision of bailing on Dean tonight.

EIGHTEEN
DEAN

Jared was almost done packing up the van, and I was waiting for him out back behind the bar. My brain continued to go over every interaction Al and I had tonight. She seemed annoyed about Sarah, which sucked. But if she was a little jealous, then that meant she was into me, right? It seemed like she was feeling me when we were on the dance floor...right before she ran away from me as fast as she possibly could.

I cursed under my breath. How into me could she be if she was that eager to get away from me?

"Can I get a little help here?" Jared stood at the door struggling to balance an amp and several heavy chords.

"Shit, my bad." I rushed to grab the amp from his hands, and we loaded the rest of the stuff into the van.

"That was awesome. Did you see how packed it was in there?" Jared asked as we both settled into our seats.

"It was awesome," I agreed.

"Can I get a little more excitement from my best friend?"

"Sorry, I'm just beat. It was great. Probably the best show I've seen to date."

Jared took his eyes off the road for a minute and assessed me. "Surprised to see you're going home alone, since I saw you with two girls tonight." He smirked and winked at me. "Or maybe that was the problem."

"I tried to blow Sarah off, but she kept hanging around." I dragged my hand across my face, feeling exasperated. "It was going pretty good with Al at the end, but I don't know. She bailed pretty fast. I'm definitely not as irresistible as everyone seems to think I am."

"Maybe." Jared considered. "Or maybe it's because her friend has been talking her ear off about how you're just using her for sex."

I scoffed and glared at him. "Tiff? I doubt she would phrase it like that."

Jared shrugged. "However she's phrasing it, she's warning Al all about your past. It's probably freaking her out. Not every girl wants to be a notch in your bedpost, dude."

"It's not even like that," I insisted. I knew very well that it actually *could* come across exactly like that.

That could be why Al left in such a hurry. She probably thought I wanted to take her home. I mean, I kind of did want to take her home. But that's beside the point. I wouldn't have pressured her to do anything she wasn't comfortable with. She probably also thought if we did do anything that I'd never call her again afterward.

"Tiff was right to warn her," I muttered. "I'm not boyfriend material. I should just leave the girl alone. I've got enough on my plate right now. The new restaurant is supposed to be open in a few weeks, and my hands are completely full with that."

"Dude, you're so full of shit."

"Excuse me?" I hit him in the shoulder but not hard enough that it would affect his driving.

He laughed at my lame shot and continued to tell me things I didn't want to hear.

"You could make time if you wanted to. I've never seen you this hung up on a girl before. If any other woman had bailed on you, you wouldn't be giving them a second thought. You're looking for an excuse not to try because you're scared, and that's the dumbest shit I've ever heard."

I rolled my eyes. "I'm not scared. It's the truth. I can't be in a relationship. I need to focus on what I'm good at—opening this restaurant."

"Well, at least you finally said you're good at something. I'm so sick of your self-deprecating attitude when you're the coolest, smartest guy I've ever met. You deserve to be happy. Text her."

Jared's relentless need to build up my confidence made me smile.

"Maybe I will."

"Good. Now can we go back to talking about what's really important? Me and how amazing I played tonight."

NINETEEN
AL

It felt like an atomic bomb had exploded inside my head. Groaning in misery, I used a pillow to shield my eyes from the sunlight peeking through my window. Through squinted eyes, I took in the unfamiliar, bare room with light yellow walls. Wait, where was I? I shot up in a panic before remembering that I had moved yesterday and this was my new room.

My head fell back onto my pillow. Rolling over, I was thankful to find I had poured myself a glass of water and left it on my nightstand. A classic responsible-drunk move I almost always did for myself. I chugged the water like I had been trudging through the Sahara for months and grabbed my phone.

Five unread text messages. One was from Tiff letting me know that it was great to see me and that we should hang out just the two of us sometime. That was sweet of her. Maybe she and Jess not including me was all in my head.

My stomach flipped as I realized the rest of the messages were from Dean.

Dean: Had a great time with you tonight, but I wish you hadn't run off so quickly. :) Please let me know that you made it home safely.

Dean: Al?

Dean: I'm going to assume that you passed out from a drunken food-induced coma and that something terrible didn't happen to you.

Dean: Seriously, text me when you see these.

My face broke out into a huge grin. He texted me. I thought for sure I had blown it when I ran out on him last night. Suddenly, I wasn't feeling so hungover.

Al: I can confirm that I did suffer from a burrito-induced coma, but I'm alive now...barely.

Pleased, I set my phone down, only to hear it immediately vibrate on the table.

Dean: Thank God, was just about to send emergency services to check on you.

Al: You might still need to send them. I can't hear my own thoughts over this mysterious ringing in my head.

Dean: I'm sure that has nothing to do with our dear friend vodka.

Al: Vodka would never betray me like that.

Dean: I'm really glad you came. I may or may not still be thinking about how good your legs looked in that dress...

He was full-on flirting with me. What should I say back?

Should I be as forward as he's being, or should I play it cool? Ugh, I hated this shit.

Easing off the bed, I made my way to the dresser to throw on whatever I had bothered to unpack yesterday. My only option was an ancient, gigantic gray hoodie. Nothing said "I'm hungover and I don't intend to do anything this morning" like a comfortable sweatshirt I could snuggle up in.

The floorboards creaked as I headed down the wooden staircase. I hoped Cameron or Nora was already up so they could give me advice on what to say back to Dean. As I entered the kitchen, I immediately halted when I found Sean already there, holding a mug and not looking hungover in the slightest.

He gave me an awkward wave, and I couldn't help thinking he was pretty adorable with his bedhead and glasses perched on the edge of his nose.

"Morning, Al. Want some coffee? I just brewed a pot."

Sighing in relief, I plopped down on one of the mismatched barstools that lined the kitchen's peninsula. "Yes, please. I'm struggling."

He poured me a mug and set it down in front of me. I blew on the hot liquid and eagerly took a sip. It scalded the roof of my mouth, but the taste instantly made me feel more alive.

"So..." Sean shifted from foot to foot, grasping for small talk. "Did you have a good night?"

"Oh, um, yeah, totally. The band was pretty good."

"Totally..." Sean took another gigantic sip of coffee.

I followed suit, racking my brain for a conversation topic. Not the easiest thing to do when you were socially awkward and had a pounding headache. Why had I thought living with a bunch of strangers was a good idea?

"So," Sean started again. "That Dean guy couldn't keep his eyes off you."

My face grew hot. "He was still with that other girl when you and Nora left."

Sean shrugged. "True. But he was staring at you the whole time."

My blush deepened as I scanned my brain for a subject change that would take me out of the hot seat.

"Is there something going on between you and Nora?" I blurted out tactlessly.

His face went bright red, which was all the answer I needed. He set down his coffee and started to fidget with his glasses, pulling them off and rubbing the already spotless lens on his shirt.

"I guess we weren't being as subtle as we hoped. I should probably let her tell you. but since you brought it up..." He paused before continuing in a rush. "We had a *moment* a few weeks ago. We were watching a movie and one thing led to another... Anyway, it surprised us both. Ever since then, there's been so much tension and flirtatious looks between us. I want to ask her out for real, but she's hesitant to do anything about us because we live together."

"So you like each other but don't want to complicate the living situation?"

He looked flustered as he nodded.

"Well, I don't want to meddle, but figuring that out seems unavoidable. You two are always together. Trying to fight feelings isn't going to end well. I think you should tell her how you feel."

He sighed. "I know you're right. It's just that—"

Sean immediately stopped talking as Nora sauntered downstairs and entered the kitchen.

"Morning. What are you two talking about so intensely?" she asked cheerily, pouring herself a cup of coffee.

Sean looked panicked, so I interjected.

"Dean. He was flirting hard last night, and he's been texting me this morning."

Nora squealed so loud it brought my hangover back to life. "Let me see."

Sean shot me a grateful glance. I handed her my phone, and she scanned the messages.

"Ooh, he's definitely crushing. What are you going to say back?"

"Ugh, I'm not sure. Do I say something flirty back? Should I say he looked good too?"

"You three are so loud. But you should play it coy," Cameron replied from the living room.

We all glanced over to see him sprawled out on the couch, looking half asleep.

"Well, good morning, sunshine." Nora laughed. "Did you sleep out here?"

"I fell asleep watching some house-hunting show."

"What exactly do you mean by 'coy'?" I asked, puzzled.

"You have the upper hand. He wanted you last night, and you left. And now he's sending flirty texts trying to bait you? Read me the conversation."

I read him the texts.

"Okay, so to that you should reply with a wink emoji or something and leave it at that. Make him carry the conversation."

"But what if he doesn't?"

My fear of rejection was painted all over my face. Nora sat down on the stool next to me and gave me a concerned look. "Al, I don't want to upset you, but I'm curious. Why do you seem so self-conscious all the time?"

Shoot, I was only twenty-four hours into this living situation and she was already reading me like an open book. I looked at my feet before answering.

"I wasn't exactly popular growing up, and I guess that feeling of never being good enough has stuck with me."

That was an understatement. I was a social pariah in middle school and high school, but I didn't want to admit that to my new friends.

Sean's comforting voice brought me back to the present. "I can relate to not being the coolest person in high school. But you can't let those memories affect who you are today. You not being accepted had nothing to do with you and everything to do with them."

I smiled. "Thanks for saying that."

Later that night I was sitting in bed reading a book, trying to fight off the Sunday scaries. Nora, Cam, Sean, and I had spent the entire day watching bad movies and eating greasy food.

My phone dinged. Dean and I had exchanged a few more messages that morning, but I hadn't heard from him since. It wasn't like I *expected* him to text me nonstop or anything, but I felt pathetic for secretly wanting him to.

Mom: Just checking in. How are the new roommates? Feeling overwhelmed?

I rolled my eyes. Why did she always have to assume that I was feeling anxious?

Al: I already feel like they're my friends, and the place is great.

Mom: Good to hear. You're so brave.

Turning off my light, I decided it was a good idea to catch

up on some sleep. I was about to drift off when I heard my phone go off again.

Dean: Good night. :)

I fell asleep with the biggest smile on my face.

The week was flying by. It was already Wednesday, and I was counting down the days to the weekend when I would get a break from this suffocating hellhole. My boss had already come to my desk three times this week to tell me I should show more initiative like my coworkers. I'd smiled through gritted teeth and promised I would, even though I had stayed late on Monday to fix a mistake that Trent had made.

I glanced at the time on my computer.

4:35.

Only twenty-five minutes until freedom. Nora had asked Cameron and me to help after work with this independent artist exhibition she was involved with. I wasn't sure what it entailed, but I was excited to spend the evening downtown with them.

My phone buzzed, and I flipped it over to check my messages.

Dean: How's the grind?

Dean had been texting me sporadically since the show. Sometimes it was a "good morning" text. Other times it was him asking how my day was going. Occasionally, he would even send a flirtatious message. To say I was pleased would be a major understatement, but despite the frequent messages, he hadn't mentioned anything about hanging out again. With the weekend fast approaching, I was getting antsy about it, but I was too much of a coward to ask him out myself.

Al: The usual. Fantasizing about walking out the front door and never coming back. You?

Dean: Haha, hang in there. I've been assembling furniture since 5 a.m. The dining room is coming together, but I'm beat. Probably going to call it a day soon.

Al: Any exciting plans after you're done?

Dean: Nothing of notable interest. You?

Al: Helping Nora with something for a few hours downtown.

I stared at my phone for a few more minutes, but he didn't reply to my last message. That was pretty typical of him. He'd send a few short messages checking in and then nothing until he felt like checking in again. At first, it was nice to know he wanted to continue to talk to me, but after a few days of this and nothing more, I wasn't so sure what his intentions were. If this was him showing interest, then I needed more validation.

Once the clock hit five, I gathered my things to go meet Nora and Cam.

"Hey, Al. Quick question." Trent appeared out of nowhere and was leaning on my cubicle.

"What's up?"

"Can you go over all of the sheets in the pricing analysis you did? I'm not following your numbers, and Shelley wants me to do a presentation on them."

My face burned hot with anger. "It would probably be easier if I presented my own work," I responded.

"Yeah, I totally agree. It's just that I'm a little bit of a better speaker, no offense, and this has to go in front of the execs."

Frustrated, I felt the familiar feeling of angry tears welling in my eyes. I would not cry in front of him.

"Sorry, but I have to go. I've been here since seven, and it's already after five. I have plans. If you're smart enough to be chosen to present my work, then I'm sure you can figure out whatever questions you have."

I pushed past him toward the elevator, not even caring that I was being unprofessional.

"Wow, thanks a lot. Way to be a team player," he called after me.

As soon as the elevator doors closed, I allowed myself to cry a few miserable tears.

"This is seriously so impressive," Cam exclaimed.

It turned out that helping Nora had involved lugging her various sculptures and paintings up six flights of stairs. It had gone relatively smoothly other than Cam complaining the entire time that he had already done his cardio workout that morning.

We were west of downtown at this gorgeous loft space. It had an open floor plan and high ceilings with exposed beams. Nora and five other artists had managed to rent out the space for a steal. They each brought their art and chipped in on appetizers and drinks. Then they blasted the event all over social media, the goal being to get exposure and maybe sell a few pieces.

"It's so great seeing it all come together. Thanks again for helping me set up. And Al, thank you so, so much for promoting the event with your internet magic."

"It was hardly magic, but I'm happy to help." I laughed.

All I had done was taken their event link and added it to some of the popular sites that appear first when people search the internet for "things to do in Chicago" or something similar.

"No, seriously, we got way more RSVPs than we were expecting, and it's all because of your help. You should consider freelancing for small businesses. I know a ton of super-talented people that struggle when it comes to anything internet, or numbers, related."

That was an interesting thought. I had never considered my skills marketable outside of a corporate environment.

"Maybe I'll look into it."

"I'll give you some contacts. I can think of some people that would jump at the chance to get help with stuff like this."

The event ended up being a success. The space was packed with people. Nora even sold four pieces and gave her card out to several people. The other artists did pretty well for themselves too. Hours later we were tearing down the decorations and helping Nora pack up the rest of her stuff.

"I've been meaning to ask, how is it going with Dean?" Cam asked.

"I don't know. Okay, I guess?" I did not sound confident with my response.

Cam set down the sculpture he was wrapping in Bubble Wrap and folded his arms. "Spill."

"Well, he's been texting me every day, but..." I didn't quite know how to iterate the problem. Was I desperate for hoping we'd hang out again so soon?

"But what?" Nora encouraged.

I looked out of one of the large windows, feeling vulnerable. "But that's it. A few texts every day and nothing else. Shouldn't he be asking to see me again if he likes me?"

"Hmm, that is a tricky one." Cam stroked his chin. "Is he

the one reaching out to you every time, or is he just responding to your messages?"

I did a quick mental tally of the few conversations we'd had. "He reaches out to me most of the time."

Nora looked relieved. "I wouldn't worry about it, then. He wouldn't keep talking to you if there was no interest there. I would give it a few more days before you overthink it."

I nodded, genuinely appreciating the advice.

"Speaking of overthinking it, how are things with you and Sean?" Cam questioned bluntly.

"Cam!" Nora screeched, looking horrified in my direction.

"What? You two are so obvious with all of the longing, lovey-dovey gazes across the room."

"Shut up." Nora was glaring at him now.

I tried to look nonchalant, but my guilty conscience was all over my face.

"You knew?" she asked, but it sounded more like an accusation.

"If I'm being honest, I did kind of notice something between you two, and Sean confirmed it," I admitted. "But please don't be mad at him. I asked him outright."

Nora exhaled deeply before plopping onto a nearby chair. "I guess I'm silly for thinking we could hide anything. I do like him, but what are we supposed to do? I don't want either of us to have to move out, but how are we supposed to start dating when we already live together?"

Cam and I looked at each other before taking the two seats next to Nora.

"Look," I started. "It's not ideal, but there's nothing you can do about that. Start dating if it's what the two of you want. You both still have separate rooms and completely separate lives. It's not like you share a studio downtown or something. *If* things don't work out, then you can worry about that when the time comes."

Cam crossed his legs and sat back. "I love you, and I know you've lived there longer than him, but I'm picking Sean in this hypothetical separation. He does way more chores."

We all burst out laughing.

"I'm so glad the internet and some random house brought us all together." She beamed when we finally settled down.

"So it's settled. You'll tell Sean how you feel," I said, getting up.

"Not so fast." Nora shot up with me. "If I have to tell Sean how I feel, then you have to tell Dean."

"Perfect. I love this plan." Cam clapped.

I tried to hide the panic in my eyes with a smile as we all finished packing up.

TWENTY
DEAN

"Nick, what the fuck is this?" I yelled, exasperated with our lead contractor.

"Chill out. Don't worry about it. We needed to get under the floorboards to do some minor pipe work."

"'Minor pipe work'?" I gestured maniacally at the gaping hole Nick had put in our beautiful hardwood floors. "Nothing about this looks minor, Nick. We're opening in three weeks, and it looks like we're on an episode of a home renovation show."

"Get out of here, Dean. I can't work with you breathing down my neck. If I say I'll get it done, I'll get it done."

I take a deep breath in and close my eyes, willing myself to calm down. Nick hadn't let us down in the past, and there was no reason for me to believe he would now. The pressure the investors had us under was driving me insane. Eric was bringing them by any minute for a walk-through, and this was the last thing I wanted them to see.

"I trust you, Nick. Don't make me look like an idiot."

I took a moment to scan the rest of the place, trying to see it from an outsider's perspective. The paint looked great, and the exposed beams had been cleaned up. We replaced all of the light fixtures and put in a new, beautiful oak bar that took up the entire length of one side of the place. Luna Two was looking pretty fantastic, despite my stressed outbursts.

The door swung open, and Eric walked in, followed closely by Todd. Todd worked for a small real estate investment firm that had the biggest stake in our restaurants, after Eric and me. Todd was always in a suit and glued to his smartphone. He said things like "Good to see you, champ." I couldn't stand Todd.

"Hey, Deanie boy, my man. What's good?" He didn't look up while he finished a text he was furiously typing out.

"Hi, Todd," I responded in an unwelcome tone.

Eric elbowed me in the side. A silent reminder for me to be polite.

"Dean, I was just going over all of the numbers with Todd. Why don't you give him a quick tour of the place?"

I put on my best shit-eating grin. "It would be my pleasure."

After a mind-numbing hour of small talk with Todd and answering every little question he had about the opening, Eric and I were finally able to get him out the door and on his way.

"Phew, man, that was a relief." Eric patted me on the shoulder. "We killed it. The place looks great. I could tell that Todd was impressed."

"Let's just hope he runs back to his firm and sings our praises to his bosses," I muttered.

"He will. Don't worry about it. Our ass-kissing was top-notch today."

I rolled my eyes. "Having to suck up to that guy makes my skin crawl."

Eric laughed and shook his head. "Hey, Dean, I have to ask you something."

My eyebrows shot up in surprise, taking in Eric's serious demeanor. "What is it?"

"I know you're going to think it's stupid and all of this marriage stuff is crap, but I want you to be my best man."

My mouth went slightly slack before I snapped it close. Eric was my only other real friend besides Jared, so this shouldn't come as too much of a surprise. But still, I figured he'd ask one of his college friends or something.

"Are you sure, man?"

"Positive. We've been through a lot together. I would never be where I am today without you."

I scratched the back of my neck. "Well, I guess so. If you're sure."

His face broke into a grin as he pulled me in for a hug, smacking me on the back. "Thanks, man. I'll need you up there so I don't pass out from nerves." He hesitated. "Speaking of nerves, this position does involve a speech."

I waved him off. "I got this. Don't worry about it."

"Just no cynicism allowed."

"Of course, I won't. Don't be an idiot. Whatever I may think about marriage has nothing to do with you and Tiff. You both are perfect for each other. Have you two picked a date for the big day yet?"

"We have. Five weeks from Saturday."

My mouth hung open again. "Five weeks? Is she pregnant?"

Eric hit me hard in the arm, and I recoiled from pain. "Of course she's not pregnant. After we had dinner with our parents, they went into this ridiculous obsessive planning mode. Tiff and I both agreed that it sounded like an absolute nightmare. We thought about eloping but then figured something super small and intimate would be perfect for us. Just our closest friends and family. Everything is going to be super minimal."

I nodded, still in shock. "But still...that's so soon."

"Trust me, when you're in love, you'll get it. There's no point in waiting." Eric got a far-off look in his eyes that made me want to puke.

"Fat chance of that ever happening."

"Oh, right. I forgot you're planning on being alone forever." Eric playfully shoved me. "Too bad. What about Tiff's friend Al? She's pretty cute, albeit maybe too young for you."

My palms started sweating at the mention of her name. I had been texting her all week even though I knew I shouldn't. I had no time, and I would be no good for her. The rational side of my brain wasn't able to stop me from daydreaming about her smile and how much I wished she hadn't run away from me after Jared's show last weekend. Her in that tight little dress...

"I already promised Tiff I wouldn't go there. She's sick of me going after her friends."

"Do you think Al is anything like Tiff's other friends? She's different. So reserved, kind of like you. Honestly, I never really thought much about her, but as soon as I saw you two together, something clicked. I could see her for you. She's very...calm. I don't know, but I could sense a spark there."

"Okay, matchmaker. I'll be sure to tell Tiff you're encouraging this."

"I'm encouraging you to give her a real chance, not to hook up and dump her immediately."

"That's all I'm good for," I mumbled.

"Bullshit," Eric said in an annoyed voice. "You're going to

fall one day, and I'll be right there to watch you land on your ass so I can say I told you so."

"Whatever." Over this conversation, I pulled out my phone to see if Al had texted me.

"You know, that's, like, the tenth time I've seen you check your phone since we got here." Eric smiled knowingly. "Just ask her out."

Completely ignoring his statement, I rolled my eyes and shoved past him. "C'mon, help me unpack some of the boxes in the kitchen. We still have a lot of work to do."

TWENTY-ONE
AL

Al: Morning! How was your night?

I cringed inwardly as soon as I hit send.

That was the best I could come up with?

Groaning, I fell back onto my bed. I had promised myself, and Nora, last night that I would be more forward with the Dean situation, so I'd spent fifteen minutes crafting a message to send to him. I figured I could test the waters by being more available to him and work my way up to asking him to hang out. Dreading the idea of being that forward, I was still hoping he'd beat me to the punch and ask me out this weekend.

It sucked liking a guy, and I dreaded putting myself out there. Sure, I had talked to guys in the past, but the stakes always felt so low. Of course, when they stopped talking to me or told me I wasn't their type, it was hard not to take it personally. It stung, but I was always able to get over it quickly. If I was being honest with myself, I knew I had never liked any of them. I was usually forcing it because Jess was so intent on finding us boyfriends.

Flashing back, I remembered a time when Jess had convinced me that I liked someone in my computer class. We had a team project that we were working on together, and he was such a slacker. I complained to Jess about him every night. She took that to mean I was harboring feelings, and was convinced we were meant to be together. I awkwardly asked him to get drinks after our project. He seemed surprised but agreed. After a boring conversation and an awkward make-out session in his dorm room, I never heard from him again, and all I felt was a sense of relief.

Was my dating life that pathetic?

I frowned and sighed. Yes, yes, it was. I had at least ten stories just like that.

Scrutinizing my now fully unpacked closet, I selected a soft brown sweater and a pair of black jeans. My office was pretty casual, thank God, so I didn't own anything that resembled a blazer or slacks.

The old digital clock on my nightstand told me I was moving slowly this morning. Shit. I needed to be out of here in seven minutes. Now rushing, I swiped on some concealer and mascara and took the steps downstairs two at a time. I had finished stuffing a granola bar in my backpack and was about to head out the door for work when my phone vibrated.

Dean: Just worked on the restaurant until late and then hung out with some friends.

Dean: Would have been better if you were there...

I punched in my response before I could second-guess myself.

Al: Is that right? :) I guess next time you'll have to invite me.

It was almost the end of the workday, and Dean still hadn't responded to my message. Part of me felt embarrassed for being so bold. But the rational part of me knew that *he* was the one flirting with *me*, so I should feel completely justified in what I said.

Oh well. I couldn't control what he did, and everyone did warn me that he liked to date around. Stringing me along was probably just a fun game for him.

I started to pack up my stuff. Jess and Tiff were meeting me around the corner for drinks.

"Everyone, before you leave, I want to make an announcement."

My boss, Shelley, stood in front of our cubicle rows and motioned for everyone to gather around. Trent was already standing by her side. I did not have a good feeling about what she was about to say.

"I wanted to let everyone know that Trent has officially been promoted to a senior position. He's done such an amazing job around here, and is always going above and beyond."

Everyone around me gave a round of polite applause and congratulations. I did my best not to give him a death glare. Edging around the circle that had formed around Trent, I attempted to escape to the elevator.

"Oh, Al, we're all going to a company happy hour in honor of Trent," Shelley called after me.

I froze, like a deer caught in headlights.

"Sorry, but I already have plans." I tried my best to look apologetic.

Trent rolled his eyes behind Shelley's back. I fought the urge to stick my tongue out at him like we were kids fighting on a playground.

An hour later I was one margarita deep. Tiff and I were listening to Jess gush about living with Tom. Apparently, he was the most thoughtful and tidy boyfriend in existence. I found the tidy part hard to believe, since anytime he came to our old place, he always left his shoes and jacket in the middle of the floor. But I still smiled and nodded along to her stories, genuinely happy that she was so happy.

"So where is this dream man tonight?" I asked Jess jokingly.

"Playing video games with some friends." Jess made a face. "It's the one hobby I don't love, but at least he waits to do it until I'm out of the house." She sucked back her drink and motioned for the waitress to get us another round. "Speaking of men, Tiff, what's Eric up to?"

"He's at the new restaurant again. He and Dean are killing themselves trying to get the place ready in time."

Leaning down to sip the last bit of my drink, I tried to look as nonchalant as possible at the mention of Dean.

Jess seemed oblivious and gently grabbed Tiff's arm. "That must be so tough having him gone all of the time."

Tiff shrugged. "I don't mind. He loves it so much. Plus, once the place is open next month, he'll be taking time off for a mini honeymoon." She looked coyly at us, clearly anticipating a response.

Jess almost spat out her drink, and my brows knit together in confusion.

"Honeymoon?" I questioned. "Why would you be taking a honeymoon next month?"

"Because we're getting married next month!" Tiff exclaimed.

Jess and I both squealed and started asking her a million questions. She explained that both their parents put on the pressure to have this big, extravagant event, and it stressed them out. They decided to have something small and didn't want wedding planning to loom over them for a year, so they decided to do it right away.

"It's honestly so much better this way. We're getting married at the country club we met at, I'm wearing my mother's wedding dress, and Jared's band is playing. It's all coming together even better than I could have imagined." She smiled, teary-eyed. She looked so happy. "And, of course, I want you two to be there. Save the date. Since my parents were planning on spending so much money on a huge affair that isn't happening, they rented rooms for everyone."

"That sounds amazing, Tiff. Tom and I will definitely be there." Jess beamed.

"Oh, and, Al, of course, you can have a plus-one."

"That isn't neces—"

"That's pretty generous considering she doesn't have a long-term boyfriend, or even a short-term boyfriend." Jess cut me off and then snorted at her joke.

I glared at her. "Nice one, Jess. Thanks."

Tiff shot me a sympathetic glance. "You and Dean seemed pretty cozy at Jared's show the other night."

She winked at me, and I had a feeling she only brought that up because of Jess's snide remark.

"Excuse me?" Jess demanded. "Al and Dean? Eric's hot partner? That can't possibly be true."

I was getting sick of Jess's attitude. It seemed like lately after a few drinks her favorite activity was to throw every subtle dig she could think of in my direction. Ignoring her, I directed all of my attention to Tiff, who was looking at me expectantly.

"I might have a tiny crush on him," I confessed. I wouldn't normally be this forthcoming, but Tiff was so kind and the tequila was making my chest warm. "He made it seem like he wanted something to happen between us that night. Now he's been texting me every day, but I'm not sure if it means anything, because he hasn't mentioned hanging out again."

Jess looked at me, dumbfounded, before crossing her arms. "I can't believe you didn't tell me."

I rolled my eyes. "It's new. I'm telling you now. Besides, it's probably nothing."

"Let me see your phone," Jess demanded, holding out her hand.

"Jess, I'm no—"

"Al, we always share this kind of stuff. Gimme."

I reluctantly handed it over and watched as they both leaned in to dissect our conversation.

Jess and Tiff scanned the messages across the table. They exchanged a pitying look before handing my phone back.

"What's that look for?"

Tiff looked conflicted before finally answering. "I don't want to hurt your feelings, but it seems like he's leading you on."

I slumped back in my seat, deflated.

"I was worried about that," I admitted.

"You can't waste your time on this," Jess insisted. "He can tell that you have a crush on him, and he's taking advantage of it."

"Why would he keep talking to me though? I don't get it."

I thought back to the day we got lunch. It seemed like we had a connection. It felt like we were both opening up to each other.

"He likes to keep a lot of girls interested," Tiff replied, looking at me sympathetically. "He's Eric's close friend, and he is a good guy, but he's completely commitment-phobic. He's texting you because it's convenient for him to always have an option available when he wants it."

I took a big sip of my drink before slamming the glass down. "Well, this sucks."

"Forget about him. Tom has a ton of friends I can set you up with."

I forced a smile and pretended to be interested as Jess started rattling off names.

"Pass me a slice, would ya?" Cam asked from across the living room.

All of my roommates were scattered around the spacious living room. We had decided to spend Friday night at home, which involved pizza and a lot of bad reality TV. Nora and I were sitting on the floor, surrounding the coffee table. Sean and Cameron were sprawled out on the ancient, oversized leather couch.

Cam had just finished detailing the events of a particularly good date he had the previous night. So good that they had a second date planned for tomorrow.

"Wow, two dates in one week? You better be careful. You're this close to settling down." Sean held up his index finger and thumb as if to demonstrate a microscopic amount.

"Watch yourself," Cam warned, taking the slice of pizza I handed back to him.

"Must be nice to have someone that wants to take you on a date," I muttered, not keeping the self-pity out of my voice.

"Wait, are you giving up on the Dean situation already?" Nora turned to me, shocked. She glanced back at the boys before leaning in to whisper, "Don't forget about our deal."

"I know," I mouthed back. Then louder for the group, I continued. "But it's hopeless. I tried to be more forward, and he hasn't messaged me since. Plus, I was talking with my friends the other night, and they're positive that he's just stringing me along."

"That's complete bullshit," exclaimed Nora.

Cam snorted in agreement.

"No, it's not," I insisted. "My friend Tiff knows Dean. Her fiancé is basically his best friend."

"I don't care. You can't dictate your life by fear. You need to at least put yourself out there before you write him off for good." Nora launched into the rest of her speech. "I agree that he should have mentioned hanging out again, but maybe he really has been busy. Or maybe he's nervous too. Regardless of the hot and cold vibes this week, he was so attentive to you in person. You need to give this a chance, Al. You keep saying that you don't always connect with guys easily, so you need to see this through."

"Amen," Cam cheered from behind us.

"All right, all right. Geez," I responded.

"Text him right now." Cam dropped to the floor, squeezing in next to me. "Ask him to hang out tonight. If he says no and doesn't propose an alternative, then you can write him off."

Under everyone's watchful eye, I pulled out my phone. I tried my best not to feel unnerved, but my fear of being rejected was at the forefront of my mind.

Al: Hey, stranger. Any chance you want to hang out tonight?

I set my phone faceup on the coffee table, and we all hovered around it, staring intently. After what felt like hours, but was probably thirty seconds, we all sat back.

Nora gave an encouraging smile. "Let's give it a few min—"

She was interrupted by my phone dinging, notifying me of a new message. Cam and Nora both screamed in unison before immediately returning their gaze to my phone.

Dean: Hey! Would love to, but unfortunately I'm bartending at Luna tonight.

My chest deflated from disappointment. He did not propose a different time. He didn't like me. I should officially give up.

"'*Would love to,*'" Cam mocked in a high-pitched, obnoxious voice. "Screw that. If he wanted to, he would. I'm sorry, Al."

"Forget him," chimed in Sean. "You can do way better than that guy."

I smiled back at him, appreciating his need to cheer me up even if it wasn't true.

"It's fine. I already expected it." I knew they were all trying to make me feel better, but I wanted nothing more than to move on and forget this moment ever happened.

Nora mouthed, "I'm sorry," before we all went back to eating our pizza in silence. It only took a few minutes before we were all chatting and laughing about the ridiculous show we were watching.

"How are we supposed to believe that the girl who is falling over drunk and shit-talking everyone is ready to get married?" Nora shook her head.

"I like her," Cam insisted. "Without her, the show would be so boring to watch."

"I like the flight attendant. She seems so mature."

"You would say that, Sean. Leave it to you to pick the most levelheaded one."

We all laughed as Sean rolled his eyes.

I saw Nora sneak a glance in his direction, and they both beamed at each other. Maybe she had already said something to him. If they got together for real, I would be happy for them despite my unfortunate predicament of an unrequited crush.

The show we were watching might be mindless and dumb, but it did make me realize something—literally *anyone* can find someone. Here I was wallowing in self-pity, while the people that went on these shows continued to put themselves out there time and time again. How could I be all broken up about one guy when I'd hardly made any effort to meet someone over the years? I made a mental note to let Jess and Tiff know that I was open to being set up.

After another hour of watching TV, we all got off our butts to tidy up the living room, which was littered with plates and half-empty pizza boxes. I grabbed my phone, intending to plug it into a charger when I noticed I had an unread message from twenty minutes ago.

Dean: Any chance you want to stop by? I hear the bartender makes a pretty good drink.

"Dean asked me if I wanted to stop by his bar tonight," I stated in disbelief.

Nora clapped her hands in delight.

"I knew it," Cam exclaimed from the kitchen. "I told you not to write him off."

I rolled my eyes.

"Tell him you'll be there soon." Nora grabbed my hand and rushed me upstairs. "Hurry, let's pick out an outfit and fix your hair."

"I'm *not* going there by myself. That's so desperate."

"You *are* desperate," Cam insisted.

"We'll go with you." Nora clapped her hands in excitement. "I'm a terrific wing woman."

"Ugh, fine. Let me see if I can stuff my bloated pizza stomach into my jeans." Cam patted his midsection.

"I look like shit," I said in a panic.

"Nothing I can't fix," Nora exclaimed.

"Would you guys hate me if I stayed in? I'm so into this novel, and I'm almost fin—"

"Oh my God, spare us the details, Sean. Have fun with your book." Cameron tailed behind us.

Once upstairs, I took in my sloppy appearance in the full-length mirror by my closet.

I groaned. "It's hopeless."

"Leave it to me." Nora eyed me up and down.

Just ten minutes later, Nora had completely transformed my hair with dry shampoo and a curling iron. I had also thrown on a little bit of mascara and concealer to freshen up my face. As for an outfit, I settled on my typical jeans and a lightweight cropped black sweater. Nora agreed that it was not only cute but it was also a good idea to look like myself. Feedback I greatly appreciated after years of dealing with Jess trying to force me into skintight clothing that showed off what little cleavage I had.

"Let's motor, ladies," Cam called from downstairs.

TWENTY-TWO
DEAN

I glanced at the door for the hundredth time since I had texted Al to stop by. She hadn't answered me, which could mean she was blowing me off, but I had a gut feeling that she was going to walk through the door at any minute.

When she had asked to hang out tonight, I couldn't deny the feeling of satisfaction that followed. Even still, I told her I was busy and tried to leave it at that, but the gnawing feeling in my gut wouldn't let me. I wanted to see her. Screw trying to stay away. I was over that.

Sorry, Tiff. Whatever happens will happen.

The bar had picked up quite a bit, and Jared and I had a steady flow of drink orders to fill. In the middle of making an old-fashioned, I clocked a petite brunette walking in.

My face broke into a huge grin, and I waved to get Al's attention. She spotted me and gave me an adorable half smile. It wasn't until she was almost at the bar that I realized she wasn't alone. Shit, she brought her roommates. That wasn't part of my plan to charm her, but I guess I would have to work around the buffer.

"Hey," I greeted them as they all slid into their seats, and we exchanged pleasantries. "I'm glad you came," I said, directing my gaze only at Al.

"Thanks for the invite." She seemed nervous. I would have to remedy that.

"What can I get you all to drink?"

"What's good here?" Cam looked at the menu with a bored expression.

"Anything if I'm making it."

He smirked at my response. "Well, don't we love a confident man? I'll have whatever your specialty is."

"Oh, how fun. I'll have that too," Nora said cheerily.

"Um, sure, same."

"Coming right up." I grabbed three glasses and flashed them what I hoped was a charming smile.

I had a feeling that if I wanted Al to like me, getting in the good graces of these two was the way to do it. Even if I wasn't getting the one-on-one time I was hoping for, it still meant something that she showed up.

"What's going on over here?" Jared appeared at my side, leaning against the bar as I poured a dash of the sour mixer into a cocktail shaker.

"Jared, you remember Al. Nora and Cam are her roommates. They were all at your last show."

"Oh, rad. Thanks for coming. We had a great crowd that night."

"You guys were amazing," Nora gushed.

The three of them continued to make small talk while I finished up the drinks. I didn't take my eyes off Al, not even caring that I was staring. Unfortunately, she was being pretty quiet, which was not what I wanted. She seemed like the type of person that had a hard time opening up in a crowd. I slid the three drinks their way, my fingers intentionally lingering on her glass.

"Order's up."

When she went to reach for the drink, our hands brushed for a moment, and I winked at her. She gave me a little eye roll, but I noticed that her smile was genuine now.

Thirty minutes later the bar had cleared out even more, and the five of us were still talking boisterously at the bar. Turned out, I liked her friends. Cam's demeanor was bone-dry, and hysterical, and Nora was unique and very optimistic. Al was meshing well with Jared too. While the three of us chatted away, he took a more one-on-one approach with her and asked her questions about herself. I'm not sure why it pleased me that my best friend was taking an interest in getting to know her, but it did. A lot.

Without any warning, Cam slammed his empty glass onto the bar and sprung out of his chair. He grabbed Nora's elbow and dragged her away.

"Oof, Cam, what're you do—"

"Well, this has been fun, but we need to get going. It's getting late after all." He started backing away with Nora in tow. "I'm assuming that the drinks are on the house. Al, we'll see you at home."

Al's eyebrows shot up in surprise as her friends practically sprinted out of Luna.

"Wow, subtle." I chuckled and shot Jared a look to make himself scarce too. He got the message and pretended to look busy at the bar computer.

She groaned, but her smile was still there. "Subtlety is not one of Cam's strengths."

I scanned the sparse restaurant and noticed an empty booth at the back. "Hey, the bar is pretty dead. Want to have a drink with me at a booth? I'll even bring some breadsticks."

"Sold."

Leading her to the table, I let my hand rest on her lower back. I motioned for her to have a seat and leaned down to whisper into her ear. "I'm kind of glad your chaperones left."

"Oh, um—yeah. They just came—they wanted to get a drink, so... These booths are comfortable."

She didn't even try to finish her lame excuse, which made me chuckle.

I ran into the kitchen and grabbed a basket of bread, hitting the bar on my way back to grab an open bottle of wine.

"So," she started nervously as I handed her a glass. "How's the new restaurant coming?"

I leaned in and swiped a piece of a breadstick. "It's coming along, but the whole thing is a shit show. The contractor keeps finding all of these issues that need to be fixed, and our main investor won't take any excuses. It's getting kind of intense, to be honest. I'm ready for all of the setup to be over so we can just be open. That's the part of the business that I enjoy, seeing everyone flood in and love the place. All of the numbers, schmoozing, and deadlines I could do without."

She grinned and fidgeted with her glass. "That kind of seems like a pretty big part of the business."

"That's why I have Eric."

"How did the two of you get into business together anyway?"

"It's a long story." I proceeded to tell her everything. From meeting Eric at the country club, to him promoting me, to opening Luna and eventually taking him on as a partner. She had her elbows on the table, leaning in with her chin resting in one hand.

"Wow, that's amazing that you started this place all on your own."

"Well, like I said, I needed Eric's help."

"But still, I can't imagine going off on my own and starting something from nothing like that. It's impressive."

I broke eye contact and scratched the back of my neck. "Well, it's not that hard to go off on your own when you've pretty much always been on your own."

"What do you mean?" Her eyebrows knit together, and she leaned in even closer, her small knee bumping into my leg. I fought the urge to put my hand there.

"It's a long, depressing story," I said with as much lightheartedness as I could muster. I typically did not bring up my family to anyone. Let alone a girl I hardly knew. "My dad was a piece of work. He lacked compassion and probably couldn't even define the word 'empathy.' He talked down to my mother and me my whole life."

Al winced and reached across the table to grab my forearm. She gave a small squeeze. "What was your mom like?"

"My mom...she was kind of a shell of a person, if I'm being honest. By the time I was born, he had done such a number on her that all she ever did was sit idly by. She never wanted to do anything that might upset him. She always told me to be quiet and behave. Maybe then we would avoid the stings of his lashing out. She died when I was thirteen, and then I became my father's sole punching bag."

I was hesitant to glance up, dreading the pity I assumed that I would see in Al's eyes. This was exactly why I chose never to speak of my upbringing. When I finally met her clear brown eyes, I saw that they were devoid of pity but instead held a sadness of their own.

"Some people should never be parents," she said matter-of-factly.

My eyes bore into hers, begging her to continue.

"My dad left when I was six. He ran off to Vegas with some woman. I barely remember him at all except that I used to hide in my room when he and my mom would get into fights."

She was clasping her hands together tightly and not meeting my eyes. Clearly, I wasn't the only one uncomfortable being vulnerable. Without thinking, I grabbed her hand. My hand engulfed her delicate one as I gave her a reassuring squeeze.

"My mom is amazing though. She always worked so hard to make sure I had more options than she did." She hesitated before continuing. "I never told her this, but I actually met up with my dad at some shitty diner right after I left for college. Apparently, he had moved back to the Midwest and remarried some younger woman with a few kids. He showed me pictures of his stepkids and bragged about them as if they were his own. He didn't ask me one question about myself and even asked me to pay the bill. It was surreal sitting across from him, this man that was responsible for creating half of me...he was just a stranger. I was too embarrassed to ever tell my mom about it."

Her voice was thick with emotion. It made me wince. I hadn't known Al long, but it was clear to me that she was fragile, and now I understood why. To think her asshole father had treated her that way made me want to hunt him down and punch his face in.

"Why did you even go meet him?"

"I don't know. I guess I've always had this fear of rejection. I never fit in at school, and I always traced it back to him. Was something inherently wrong with me? Even my dad didn't like me." She looked down at the table. "I guess I thought seeing him again would be closure, but it kind of just reopened old wounds. It sucked knowing he had a new family that he chose to stick around for."

My blood boiled as I leaned in. Still holding her hand, I pulled her toward me. "Never think like that. If he can't see how great you are, that's on him. But never let him define your worth, because let's face it, he's a piece of shit."

She smiled and wiped a lone tear away. "I guess I should say, 'Right back at you.'"

Realizing what I had just said, I chuckled. "We're kind of a mess, aren't we?"

Al laughed, and I was grateful for the fracture in the tension. She was breaking down all of my walls like they were made of dust.

TWENTY-THREE
AL

"I swear, it was a casual bar and grill, and it was only five on a Tuesday. There were a bunch of older couples eating an early dinner. Jess had plastered me with shots already and was trying to force me to eat a burger. I was so drunk that I fell out of my chair and was completely sprawled out in the middle of the floor. I hit the ground so hard I could barely stand up, and Jess was trying to convince the waiter that the stool was slippery or something ridiculous like that. Anyway, he kicked us out, and I've been too embarrassed to return, which is a bummer because they actually did have good burgers."

I covered my face, feeling ashamed of my former self, but also enjoying that I was making Dean laugh so hard. We had been chatting in the booth for what felt like minutes, but I'm sure it had been hours.

"That's too good," he finally choked out. "You know you're supposed to go to a club or something, right? Not to the early-bird special."

"We were doing a bar crawl," I countered, pretending to be defensive. "Okay, hotshot. Let's hear about your amazing twenty-first birthday. That is, if you can remember that far back."

"Ouch, that one hurt." Dean smiled, nudging my leg with his knee under the table. "Let's see, I think Jared and I just went out with a few other people from the country club. I can't say anything particularly memorable happened to me."

"You're pretty close with Jared." I meant it as a question, but it came out as a statement.

"He's my best friend. We've known each other since we were little kids, and he's gotten me through a lot of rough times."

"That must be nice to have such an old friend."

"It is. He knows me better than anyone else." He looked at me intensely. "What about your friend Jess? You talk about her a lot."

"We met in college, but she was my first actual friend. We've always done everything together, but it's felt different ever since she started dating her boyfriend."

"She doesn't have much time for you?"

I thought about the best way to articulate what I was feeling. "Well, yes. That's true. We don't spend as much time together. But also, I've been realizing lately that I've kind of been letting Jess run my life. It was so easy to go along with whatever she suggested and become friends with the people that she had met. Ever since we stopped living together, I've realized I haven't been fully myself. I've been adapting to whatever mold she made." I looked at Dean, not feeling self-conscious for once. "Does that make any sense?"

He nodded and leaned forward. "It does."

"And don't get me wrong, I still love Jess. But I've felt more myself since moving in with my new roommates than I have in years."

We continued to talk about everything and anything, down

to our favorite movies. It felt like no time had passed, but when I finally looked up, I noticed that Luna had completely emptied and Jared was stacking chairs onto tables.

"Oh, shoot. I didn't realize it was so late. I should probably get a cab home."

Dean waved off my suggestion like it was the most ridiculous thing he'd ever heard. "I'll drive you. Let me give Jared the keys to lock up."

Dean was driving me home. I willed my body not to freak out.

Did this mean anything? Was he going to ask if I wanted to go to his place instead? We had spent hours talking, and he had been touchy the entire time. His leg was constantly brushing against mine. He had even grabbed my hand at one point. It had to mean something. I'd already mentally prepared myself for this—I was not going to freak out and bolt like last time. I wanted something to happen between us, even if it was short-lived. I was sick of living my life on the sidelines. No one had ever made my stomach flip the way Dean did.

"After you."

My mind snapped back to the present, and I realized Dean was holding the door open for me. I smiled up at him in what I hoped was an inviting way as we walked over to his van. The temperature had dropped quite a few degrees since I arrived, and my thin sweater wasn't doing much for me.

"You're cold." Dean fished around in the back seat before producing a dark-gray zip-up sweatshirt. "Here, wear this."

"Thanks." I shrugged the sweatshirt on, trying my best to play it cool when all I wanted to do was bury my face in the fabric and inhale Dean's intoxicating scent.

The entire drive to my house my body was buzzing with excitement. He was gripping the steering wheel with his left hand while his right arm was resting on the center console, his hand dangerously close to brushing against my thigh. It took all of my willpower not to look up at him to see if he was sneaking glances at me.

After a few tension-filled minutes, we arrived at the front of my house. My excitement turned to disappointment as I realized Dean was not planning on propositioning me tonight. I cringed at just how resistible I must be for him not to want to hook up with me at all.

I opened my door, eager to remove myself from this feeling that felt very similar to rejection. When I finally met his eyes, I saw that they were dark and intense.

"Thanks for driving me home." I licked my lips, begging him to close the gap between us and kiss me. I would have made the first move if I wasn't so irrationally afraid that he'd turn away in disgust.

After a few excruciating seconds of silence, he nodded abruptly and finally said, "No problem. I'll talk to you later."

Disappointed, I hung my head, feeling stupid that I thought he was going to make a move. I hopped out of the car and slammed the door shut behind me.

I was about to start ascending the rest of the stairs when I heard Dean mutter a curse under his breath.

"Al, wait!" he shouted.

I looked up to see him jumping out of his van and barreling toward me. He took a few long strides determinedly in my direction and stopped right in front of me. He purposefully grabbed my face and searched my eyes questioningly for a few moments before capturing my mouth with his.

His soft lips moved slowly over mine as a warmth began to grow in my chest. My mouth parted slightly in a silent moan, and he took full advantage by slipping inside, teasing my tongue with his.

His hands traveled from my face down my body. They

moved over my torso, pausing at the sides of my breasts before finally descending to my hips. His strong hands grabbed onto my sides, and he pulled my body into his. The friction between our bodies was almost too much for me to bear. It had been ages since the last time a guy had touched me, and it had *never* felt like this.

I threw my arms around his neck and kissed him even deeper. I started to grind my body into his, desperate to shed these layers and feel his skin on my skin. Dean groaned before suddenly breaking away from our entanglement. He took a step backward, breathing heavily. I was left alone on the steps, feeling cold from his absence.

"Sorry, I didn't mean to get carried away."

I tilted my head, giving him what I hoped was a very confused look. I was still a little too wound up to attempt speaking at that moment.

He took a step forward and planted a lingering kiss on my lips. "Good night, Al."

He left me standing there on my front step, trying to process if what had just happened between the two of us was real or my imagination.

"Hey, what are you doing tomorrow?"

I looked up to see Dean back in his van, talking to me through the open passenger-side window.

"N-nothing," I stammered, my lips still tingling from the kiss we'd shared.

"I'll pick you up at noon."

I checked my reflection for the hundredth time that morning. Huffing in frustration, I ripped off the shirt I was wearing and began digging through my drawers again. Half of my clothes were strewn around the room, since I had tried on every outfit I owned twice already. I thought about texting Dean to try to gauge the dress attire for today, but Nora told me that would be crazy and that the event implied casualness. Knowing she was right, I bit my lip and stared down at my phone, still tempted to ask.

Turned out what Dean was picking me up at noon for was an outdoor BBQ. He didn't give me many details aside from that.

I picked up my olive-green overall shorts that I had already tried on and cast aside. Jess always said they made me look childish, but I thought they were cute and the color complimented my tan skin. Plus, it was probably the last warm day we were going to get before fall officially set in. I threw them on along with a white shirt. I grabbed a sweater in case it cooled off later and rushed out of my room, determined not to change again.

Once downstairs I began pacing around the living room. My roommates had all gone out to brunch, leaving me alone to be nervous until Dean picked me up. I had another fifteen minutes to go, but there was no way I could concentrate on anything else. I wondered who would be there and cursed myself for not asking. I tended to always clam up a little bit around groups of new people.

Vacuuming the floors was one of my chores this week, so I decided what better way to distract myself than lug around a twenty-pound vacuum. I made quick work of the downstairs and was borderline out of breath when I checked the time again. He should be here any minute. I raced upstairs to check my reflection one last time. My forehead was glistening, so I took a tissue to pat it down.

There was a knock at the door, and I actually screamed out of surprise. He must be early. I forced myself to walk calmly back downstairs and toward the door. My heart felt like it was going to beat out of my chest. With one last deep breath, I swung open the door.

"Hey," I said, stepping outside to join him.

I tried to keep my body language open in case he wanted to go in for a hug or something.

"Hey." He grinned, gesturing for me to go first down the stairs. He made no move to hug or kiss me, which made me the tiniest bit disappointed, since yesterday his hands were all over me.

We got in his car, and he spent the short drive giving me more details about the day. He informed me that Eric and Tiff would be there, along with Jared and his new girlfriend, Janelle. The BBQ itself was at their investor Todd and his wife's house.

"Todd can be a little snobby," Dean warned me.

Nodding, I couldn't help taking note that it was all couples today. Did that mean something that Dean had invited me? Surely it must. It was only going to be his close friends and someone important from the restaurant. I bit back a grin.

When we pulled into a driveway just outside the city limits, I thought we must have made a wrong turn. The brick house that lay before us was massive. It even had a circle driveway with a fountain out front. My eyes widened as I looked to Dean for an explanation.

He shut off the car and shrugged. "Some people have money and are classy, like Eric. And some people"—he gestured to the McMansion—"are tacky as shit." He took me by surprise and grabbed my hand. "Ready?"

I nodded and tried to give him a sincere smile, but I knew that it didn't reach my eyes. I was already mentally filing through all of the small-talk topics I could think of. At least Tiff would be there.

Once we were at the oversized front door, he made a move

like he was going to open it but then turned around. He leaned down and gently grabbed the back of my neck before pulling me in for a sweet kiss. He lingered for a few moments before pulling away. "I should have done that when I picked you up."

I smiled, this time genuinely. "Yes, you should have."

He grabbed my hand and gave it a quick squeeze. "Please don't worry about impressing anyone, just be yourself."

"I'm not worried," I lied.

His eyebrows rose, and he gave me a look that told me he didn't believe me, but I was grateful that he didn't push it.

He led me through a grand marble entryway and straight through a massive living room and kitchen. I couldn't help marveling at what must have been twenty-foot ceilings. At the back of the house, there was a sliding glass door that led to a large fenced-in backyard.

Everyone was already there. The patio setup had several different seating options. Jared was at the tiki bar mixing up a drink and smiling at a pretty redhead who must have been Janelle. Tiff was sitting in a lounge chair laughing with a very well-dressed woman. I was assuming that the woman must be Todd's wife. She seemed so much older than me, probably due to the fancy linen pantsuit she was wearing, but her flawless complexion revealed that she was close to Dean's age.

Eric was by the grill talking animatedly about something with a shorter guy dressed in a polo shirt and khakis. Must be Todd. Eric spotted us and waved. "Hey, nice of you to join us."

"You said noon-ish. This is 'ish.'" He threw his strong arm protectively over my shoulder. "Al, you haven't met Todd and Lindsey yet, our gracious hosts."

"Nice to meet you, Al," Todd said, much louder than necessary. "Funny, I think that's my mechanic's name."

Lindsey just nodded in my direction before looking back at Tiff.

My cheeks felt hot. Clearly, I was the outsider here. Tiff, thankfully, smiled at me and tried to get up out of her seat, but Lindsey grabbed her arm. "Wait, Tiff. I *have* to show you where the pool is going in."

Tiff shot me a sympathetic look and mouthed, "Be right back," before following Lindsey to the far end of the yard.

"Hey, you two, come meet Janelle," Jared said, waving us over.

"Let me grab a beer first." Dean steered us to a built-in cooler at the edge of the patio.

He lifted the lid and eyed the selection.

"So." I took a water bottle for myself. "You haven't met Jared's girlfriend before."

"Nah." He grabbed a beer before letting the cooler lid drop. He glanced behind us to make sure we weren't in earshot before continuing. "Jared tends to bring new girls around pretty often. It's hard to keep up." He cracked open his beer and took a swig. "I know it's a terrible thing to say, but sometimes I don't even bother to remember their names."

I tried my best to shrug off that comment, but it rubbed me the wrong way considering that everything Dean was saying about Jared were things I had heard about *him*.

"Well, it seems like he likes her. He's calling her his girlfriend and introducing her to his friends." I tried to keep the defensiveness out of my voice.

"Trust me, you don't know him like I do. He always introduces us to whatever girl he's dating. He thinks he's falling for her, and then the next day"—he snaps—"he thinks he's falling for someone new."

"Oh."

"Come on, let's go mingle." Dean grabbed my hand and squeezed it as he pulled me toward the rest of the group.

About an hour later, I was finally feeling more comfortable. Although Dean's comments about Janelle rubbed me the wrong way, I made a conscious decision to push his words to the back of my mind and focus on having a good time.

The guys were all playing yard games, which left the girls on the patio to make small talk. Normally, this would be my nightmare, but Janelle turned out to be pretty cool. She did social media work for a tech startup, so we commiserated for a bit about awful coworkers.

I tried to ask Tiff questions about the wedding, but it was tough with Lindsey interrupting her every five seconds.

"Oh, I could *never* imagine having such a small wedding. Ours was so extravagant. It was the best day of my life, and people are *still* talking about it." Tiff smiled politely at her but would sneak a glance at me every once in a while, which made it clear that she thought Lindsey's attitude was snobby.

"I love that you're doing a small wedding. It's going to be so much more memorable with only your close family and friends there," I chimed in.

Lindsey shrugged. "I guess a beautiful wedding isn't for everyone."

Tiff rolled her eyes and mouthed, "Thank you," at me when Lindsey's eyes were diverted.

"Um, Lindsey, is there a bathroom I could use inside?" I didn't have to go very badly, but I was desperate for a break in this conversation.

She waved toward the sliding glass door. "Just head inside. It's the room with the toilet."

My cheeks burned at her dismissive comment, and I bit on my tongue to keep from saying something rude back. Dean and his friends were so nice and down to earth. It was hard to imagine them hanging out with Lindsey and Todd.

Through the ornate kitchen was a short hallway that I assumed led to a bathroom. I opened the first door on my left only to be met with an office setup. I was about to back out of the room when I saw a few funky paintings hanging on the wall. They immediately reminded me of Nora, so I took a few steps toward them to inspect. I was going to sneak a picture to show her later when I heard voices enter the kitchen.

TWENTY-FOUR
DEAN

"I'm sorry, but it's hard to keep track when you constantly bring a new girl to everything." Todd laughed, clasping my shoulder.

The guys had come inside to get more burgers to throw on the grill, and Todd was managing to piss me off per usual. He had been giving me a hard time about Al being "young and less mature" the entire time we were playing bags outside. I kept giving Eric a warning glance that I might have to punch him in the face at some point this afternoon.

Todd opened the refrigerator and started rummaging through it. "And I still can't believe she's so young. Good for you, I guess."

"She's only a few years younger than us." I clenched my fists, trying not to let his comments get to me.

"So probably too young to be looking for anything serious," Todd retorted. "All I'm saying is that it would be nice for you to meet someone and settle down like the rest of us. It's annoying having to get to know these girls just for you to bring a new one along."

I felt a strong hand on my shoulder grounding me. I turned

to look at Jared, who was giving me a warning look not to do anything dumb. I looked to Eric for support but was surprised to find him staring at the floor, rubbing the back of his neck.

"Eric, a little help here would be nice."

He shrugged. "Well, it would be nice if you met someone. I know that you hate the idea of a girlfriend, but I feel like I could invite you to more stuff if you were part of a couple. Tiff is always wanting to do a couple's game night or some bullshit, and I'd rather you be there than the boring-ass guys her sorority sisters are with."

There was a moment of silence.

"You guys know I have a hard time getting close to anyone."

I wanted to tell them that Al was different, that I actually might like her. But was that even true? Sure, I was hung up on her. Yes, I couldn't stay away from her. I still didn't know if that made me ready to commit to someone.

I couldn't make eye contact with them or say anything more with Todd in the room. Frustrated, I set my beer down on the counter a little too hard. "And why are you giving me grief all of a sudden? I've been like this since you met me. Jared is even worse. Why don't you take digs at him for once?"

"News flash, I've been dating Janelle for a month. You can be in denial all you want, but I have a girlfriend now." Jared glared at me, and I felt bad for trying to throw him under the bus with me.

"Deanie boy, it's time to grow up a little. We're just saying this because we want you to find someone special. Let's face it, Al seems like a nice girl, but she's not the one you're going to settle down with." Todd's smug face looked extra punchable.

I didn't know if I was angrier that he was commenting on my life, or that he couldn't keep Al's name out of his mouth. If his company wasn't giving us tons of money, I would have told him off years ago.

"I'm going to get some air."

Not waiting for a response, I stalked back outside and immediately went to a couch in the corner to cool off. My love life was none of their business. So what if I never settled down? Thinking about that immediately brought Al's face to the forefront of my mind. She *was* different. We had talked about things that I never shared with anyone. And she actually understood me to a certain degree. I understood her too.

Thinking of Al made me scan the yard for her. I didn't see her talking with the girls.

"Man, I thought we were grilling burgers, not you." My thoughts were interrupted as Jared plopped on the couch next to me. "I can't believe you have to deal with that asswipe on a regular basis."

"Just until Luna Two is open. He'll hardly be around after that. I'm counting down the seconds, believe me."

"Anyway." Jared shifted in his seat. "I wanted to make sure you weren't letting him get to you."

"I'm not," I responded in an angry tone that proved I was.

"I don't want you second-guessing anything either."

My eyebrows knit together. "What are you talking about?"

"I've known you the longest. Believe me, I understand why you are the way that you are. I know why you have a hard time with the idea of a relationship...but I also know that I've never seen you act this way. You helped the girl move, for Christ's sake." Jared sat back and eyed Janelle. "It's nice having someone that's in your corner. I don't want you to give up a chance at being with someone just because you're so programmed to flee at the first sign of something serious."

I sucked in a breath, realizing that the thought of leaving Al was giving me a very large pang in my chest and a lump in my throat.

"I guess it could be nice."

"It's the best. She's there when I get off work. We make dinner together. She listens when I want to vent about something. She's excited when I'm excited...it's the best. And I want that for you. Just try, okay?"

"Maybe," I muttered.

TWENTY-FIVE
AL

My cheeks burned as I waited for the kitchen to clear out. I felt terrible that I was eavesdropping, but I also felt too awkward to come out now, after hearing them discuss how I wasn't good enough for Dean.

"I will say that Al is a hot piece of ass," I heard Todd whisper to someone before whistling. "Good for Dean that he can still get with a twenty-three-year-old."

Someone murmured something inaudible, and I took a huge breath as I finally heard the slider door close. I waited a few more seconds until I was sure the coast was clear and then lunged into the hallway. Shooting down the hall, I finally found the bathroom a few doors down from where I had been trapped.

The mirror revealed a bright red face with bloodshot eyes. Being an attractive crier was not a trait that I possessed. I took deep breaths with my eyes closed, willing my puffy face to retreat. I splashed some cold water to help the process along.

After a few minutes, my face had returned to normal, but I was still dreading reentering the backyard. Everyone must think I was getting sick in here or something, but I couldn't muster up the energy to care. They all didn't seem to think much of me to begin with.

I took one last look in the mirror and practiced faking a smile before heading back through the kitchen and outside.

"Did you find it okay?" asked Tiff, now standing at the grill with the guys. "I was about to go in and check on you."

"Yeah, thanks."

Dean finally looked my way, and I thought I saw a brief flash of concern in his eyes. Maybe he realized I might have overheard them.

I gave him the most genuine smile I could muster. He returned it, looking relieved, and went back to flipping burgers.

I went back to the cooler to retrieve another drink. With the lid open, I stared blankly at the contents. My mind was zoning out, back to the conversation I had heard.

"Mind if I join you?" Jared materialized at my side.

I forced a smile that didn't reach my eyes. "Of course."

"I'm glad we're finally getting a chance to talk. You've really done a number on my boy, huh?" He wiggled his eyebrows suggestively.

My brain failed to send a signal to my mouth to speak. I was still reeling from the embarrassment I felt at almost being a notch in Dean's bedpost.

Jared must have mistaken my silence for coyness. "Come on, you must realize how much he likes you. Ever since that day he helped you move and you came to my show, he's been mentioning you. And I've noticed him constantly texting you, which, trust me, is rare."

I shifted from foot to foot, uncomfortable with the conversation. Maybe an hour ago, I would have been thrilled at this revelation, but now I knew that it was all a line. "We're just hanging out," I said.

Jared threw back his head and laughed. "Now that sounds like something Dean would say."

"I've heard he's quite the serial dater." I tried and failed to keep the bitterness out of my voice.

Jared's smile fell as he registered my chilly demeanor. "I don't know what you heard, but I can't lie, Dean has dated a lot in the past." He fidgeted with the drink he was holding. "But I swear to you, I've never seen him this excited about anyone before."

A murmur of hope tugged at my heart, but it wasn't enough to erase what I had overheard in the kitchen. If Dean had felt that way, wouldn't he have stuck up for what we had? Instead, he stood there and let his friends talk about how young and not special I was.

"Thanks for saying that, but I know there isn't anything serious between us." I finally grabbed another water and took a sip.

"Look." Jared turned so his back was to the rest of the group and he was facing me. "Dean is my best friend. I know that you know he hasn't had the easiest life growing up. After his mom died, he didn't have anyone that was there for him. I tried my best, but it was hard to get through the walls he'd built up. And his dad is such an asshole." His face hardened at the mention of Dean's father. "My point is that he's hardly had any good relationships in his life, let alone romantic ones. He doesn't want to let anyone in only to be disappointed."

Jared searched my face, but I wasn't giving anything up.

"Please, just be patient with him. He might not know how to navigate a relationship, but I promise you he likes you—a lot—and he's trying."

At his last plea, my chest finally deflated. "I like him too," I admitted. "But unfortunately for him, I also don't know how to navigate a relationship."

Jared grinned and lightly bumped my shoulder with his fist. "You two can figure it out together."

After the talk with Jared, I was able to put on a brave face and mingle for a few more hours with everyone. I still didn't feel confident after what I had overheard, but I put it in the back of my mind for now. It helped that Dean was very attentive the rest of the time. He made me a plate of food, saved me a seat so I could sit next to him, and even held my hand when we were sitting next to each other on the outdoor couch.

The sun was getting low in the sky when Dean finally whispered to me, "You ready to head out?"

"Sure, I'm pretty beat."

We stood up and started saying our goodbyes, which turned into everyone's cue to leave as well.

Tiff caught me by the arm on the way out while Dean was discussing something with Eric. "I feel like I hardly got to talk to you."

"I know. I wish I could have heard more about the wedding. It was hard to get a word in."

"It's hard for anyone to get a word in with Lindsey monopolizing the whole conversation," she whispered, and rolled her eyes.

I laughed. "I'm so glad you said that. I was worried you two were friends or something."

"Oh God no. I have to put on an act for Eric's sake." She chuckled. "We didn't even invite them to the wedding, but I was too much of a chicken to tell that to Lindsey in person. I'll let Eric deal with that later."

"I don't blame you. So do you have everything figured out?"

"I think so. It's going pretty smoothly, minus Eric's parents trying to invite all of their friends and double the guest list."

"I guess they probably don't have 'small' and 'intimate' in their vocabulary."

"Definitely not." She giggled. "I'm glad you came with Dean today. I know I've been super annoying warning you off of him, but I actually think you two could be really great together."

"Oh, um, thanks. I wouldn't get your hopes up though."

"It's hard not to. It would be so amazing if you two started dating. We could go on double dates and hang out when Dean and Eric are always together."

I smiled. "I would love that."

"Really? I'm so glad." She looked away, as if unsure, before continuing. "I'm embarrassed to admit this, but sometimes I worry that you don't like me that much or something. Anytime I do something with Jess, she always says you're busy. I thought maybe that was an excuse to avoid me."

My blood started to simmer. Was that why I was never invited to hang out with Jess and Tiff? Because Jess was lying and saying that I was busy? I was getting fed up with her.

"That's not it at all. I would love it if we could hang out more. Maybe even just the two of us."

Tiff beamed. "That would be amazing. I'll text you."

By the time we got in Dean's car, the sun was about to set. I was a little drowsy, and my chest felt warm, the kind of feeling you can only get after spending an entire day outside on a warm early fall day.

"Thanks for inviting me." I gave Dean a sincere, albeit tired, smile.

With one hand on the wheel, he used his other to grab my left hand and bring it to his lips. "Any chance you want to see my place? We could watch a movie or something."

"Sure." I tried my best to keep the nerves out of my voice.

We drove in silence for a few minutes before I started to replay the day in my head. I wanted to let go of what I had overheard, but it was still weighing on me. I took a deep breath and blurted it out.

"I'm sorry, but I overheard you talking in the kitchen at the party. I didn't mean to, but I was trying to find the bathroom."

Dean whipped his head around to look at me, his eyebrows drawn together in concern. I could see his eyes mentally reviewing every conversation he had that day. "What did you overhear?"

"The stuff about you dating a lot and how your friends want you to meet someone older and special." I was talking so fast, eager to be done with this conversation. "I know that you hate commitment. Everyone has made that crystal clear. And I know we're just hanging out and that this is casual, but it still kind of sucked to hear." I mumbled the last words. I hated being vulnerable, but I couldn't go back to his place without getting this off my chest.

Before I could say anything else, Dean whipped the car off to the side and pulled into a street parking spot on the side of the road.

"What are you do—"

"I'm so sorry you overheard that. I'm such an idiot." Dean cut me off and scooped up both my hands in his. "Todd is an asshole. Ignore everything that came out of his mouth today. I can't stand that guy. I should have stuck up for you, but..." He paused, searching my eyes for something. "I guess I'm used to always having to suck up to Todd. I should have drawn the line though."

He stared pleadingly at me.

I opened and closed my mouth, unsure of what to say next.

He brought my hands up to his lips and kissed both of them.

"So you could see this maybe going somewhere?" I winced at how pathetic and needy I sounded.

Dean exhaled and dropped my hands to use his to rub his eyes. My fingers immediately felt cold from his absence.

"I'm not sure what you want me to say here. This is the most I've tried for any girl in my entire life. I can't make any promises, but I like you." He looked at me, begging me to understand. "Can't we just see what happens?"

My brain was working overtime trying to process his words. It wasn't exactly the romantic declaration I was hoping for. He did say he liked me though. That had to count for something, right? I couldn't ignore the gnawing feeling in my gut that I was about to get hurt. Bad.

"Your silence is killing me here."

"Sorry," I replied, still unsure of what to say next.

"Please don't apologize to me right now. I'm the biggest asshole on the planet."

"Definitely not the biggest," I muttered.

He caught the implication in my tone. "Was there anything else you wanted to tell me?"

"Just that..." I paused, embarrassed to replay this last part again. "I overheard Todd say that I was a 'hot piece of ass' and good for you for getting with me." My shoulders slumped as I said the words out loud.

Dean's eyes darkened. "I'll kill him."

"Please don't tell him," I begged. "It's humiliating. I just want to pretend like it never happened."

"You should not feel humiliated." His words were forceful. "I promise I won't bring up that you mentioned anything to me, but I will be having a little talk with Todd. You can bet on that."

His defensive demeanor made me feel slightly better about the whole thing, so I nodded and tried to relax the stiffness between my shoulders.

"So are we good? Do you still want to come over?" His eyes looked hopeful.

"Of course." I tried to put my nerves and apprehensions out of my head. So what if he wanted to keep it casual? Wasn't that better than nothing? No guy had ever made me feel like this before. Plus, he was so freaking attractive it wasn't fair. Thinking about our kiss last night gave me a tingly feeling between my legs that I had only read about in books. I could do casual. I welcomed casual. And if he decided he wanted something more serious, then that would be welcomed too.

The plush velvet sofa felt soft underneath my fingertips. Dean's place was tastefully decorated with a mid-century modern feel to it. His walls were covered in sketches, photographs, and vinyl records. There was a large window overlooking what I assumed was the courtyard of the building, although it was hard to tell now that the sun had completely set.

Dean was in the kitchen. To my surprise, he was actually making popcorn and had already set up a movie for us to watch.

I clutched my hands into tense fists, willing the dampness of my palms to let up. I had assumed that the movie was a lame front to get me back to his place, but he seemed genuine in his desire to hang out with me. I, on the other hand, wasn't sure I could ignore the palpable tension between us as he sunk into the couch only inches away from me.

"Popcorn?" He held the bowl up, and I grabbed a handful, eager to have something to do.

Dean pressed play, and I tried to settle in and focus on the TV instead of the firm torso that smelled amazing sitting right next to me.

Fifteen minutes in, I still wasn't completely invested in the film, but my heart rate had decreased. As if sensing that I was finally comfortable, Dean set down the popcorn and slung his strong arm around my shoulders. He pulled me gently so my body would sink into his and my head could rest on his shoulder. Once again, my heart rate spiked.

"I'm sorry again about earlier," Dean whispered into my ear.

"It's okay."

"No, it's not." He kissed the top of my head. "But I'm glad you're here and didn't write me off completely like I deserve."

Looking up at him, I tried my best to assess his face. He stared down at me, his normally bright eyes appearing quite dark. The movie played completely forgotten in the background.

"Why *was* it so hard for you to tell your friends that you might like me?"

"First off, I definitely like you. A lot more than you realize." He murmured the last part so softly I almost didn't hear him. "I guess I didn't want to invite their opinions into my life."

My cheeks burned as he continued to open up. I wanted to believe him, but my internalized fear of rejection was lingering in the back of my mind, screaming to get to the forefront.

"I like you too," I whispered.

Dean leaned forward slowly, as if nervous that I would bolt and run at any moment. Gently, he cupped my chin with his fingers and brought my face closer to his. He descended on my lips with care and took his time kissing me, exploring every inch of my mouth. Our first kiss had been intense and rushed. This one felt slow and deliberate.

His mouth continued to move over mine as his hand dropped from my shoulder to my waist. He used his other hand to turn me so that our bodies were now facing each other, getting dangerously closer.

I felt his warm touch high on my thigh before he moved his fingers up, caressing the part of my leg hidden just beneath my shorts.

"Is this okay?" he whispered, still dragging his lips purposefully across mine.

"Mmm," I softly moaned in response.

Arching my back, I pushed our bodies even closer together. In response, Dean's kiss deepened as his fingers crept closer to the warmth growing in my core.

It had been ages since anyone had touched me there, and I could never remember a time when I wanted it more. I parted my legs more, begging him to touch me where I needed him to. He brushed the sensitive skin on the inside of my leg, just inches away from the heat building within me. My loose fitting shorts weren't acting as a barrier at all.

I shuddered beneath his touch, and that was all it took to set him off. He finally slid his fingers underneath my shorts and over my underwear, rubbing my growing heat softly between his thumb and finger.

He move the thin piece of the fabric to the side so he could feel me. "You're so wet," he mumbled into my mouth.

"Please touch me," I whimpered, not caring at all if I sounded desperate.

He groaned before crushing his lips to mine, his tongue exploring my own. His fingers moved expertly, rubbing me exactly where my body was begging him to. The building sensation was getting to be too much. I was desperate for a release. Just when I thought I couldn't take it anymore, Dean slipped a finger inside me. He slowly slid it in and out while still rubbing my core with his thumb.

I moaned loudly as my body caved completely into him.

He gripped my back with his other hand, supporting my weight entirely as he continued to pleasure me. He slipped a second finger inside me, and the added friction was so close to sending me over the edge. I moaned into his mouth as his fingers started to move faster, with more purpose.

His once gentle thumb rubbed me harder, and the building sensation growing within me finally rose to the top as I felt my release. My entire body gave a few shudders of pleasure before I lay slack in his arms.

Dean removed his hand from my shorts but left it resting on my upper thigh. I had ended up completely in his lap. He hugged me to his body and kissed the top of my head. Feeling shy again, I ducked my head under his chin, resting it on his chest.

"You're so sexy," he said into my hair.

My face turned a shade of crimson as I muttered a soft "Thanks."

"Don't get shy on me now." I could hear a grin playing on Dean's lips.

I finally brought my head up so I could meet his eyes. They were so warm as he stared at me.

"I don't do this often," I admitted.

Dean's grin turned devilish before he said, "Mind if I change that?"

We spent the rest of the evening pretending to watch the movie while we explored each other's bodies. My appetite for him seemed to be insatiable, and judging by his constantly roaming hands, I think he felt the same.

I was surprised that he never made a move to take off his clothes or mine.

"There's no rush," he had murmured to me.

While my desire to feel his naked body on top of mine was strong, I was relieved that we were taking this at least moderately slow.

After hours of making out on the couch, I had tried to tell him that it was getting late and that I needed to head back. He pulled me back to him and insisted that I stay. That night I fell asleep feeling content wrapped in his strong arms. The word "casual" was the furthest thing from my mind.

TWENTY-SIX
DEAN

My blank phone screen stared back at me as I tapped my pen furiously against the bar top. It had been two days since Al had spent the night, and I'd hardly heard from her since. Usually at this point, girls would be blowing up my phone asking to hang out again. It was also usually the point that I started to ice them out, but that was beside the point.

"Whoa there, tiger. What did that pen ever do to you?" Jared set down a box of unopened glassware and grabbed a box cutter to slice open the packing tape.

"Nothing," I mumbled. Breaking my trance, I started to help him unpack the glasses into the back of the bar.

Jared raised his eyebrows and looked down at my phone. "Seems like you're eager to hear from someone."

"No, I'm not." I sounded like a five-year-old and not a grown man.

"Dude, admit it. You are so hung up on her. If you just told her that then maybe you would be less distracted and could actually focus on the opening."

"I am focused. Everything is on track," I insisted.

"Is he staring at his phone again?" Eric walked through the kitchen doors with several more boxes to unpack.

"You guys need to stop."

"Come on, man. Join us in the 'happily committed relationship' club. I promise it's way more fun than you think it is," Eric responded.

"Yeah," Jared continued. "You always have someone to hang out with—"

"Someone that supports you—"

"Someone to have sex with." Jared winked at me, and Eric laughed.

I ignored them. They were wrong. I didn't care that she was being distant. We had a good time, and if she wanted to blow me off, then she was saving me the trouble.

But she wouldn't do that, right? I knew I had upset her at the BBQ, but I thought we had cleared the air. It was more than a hookup. We had shared personal shit with each other, and I didn't do that with anyone. The more I thought about our vulnerable conversations, the more her ignoring me pissed me off.

I slammed a glass down on the shelf, and it clipped the top of the bar, chipping in the process.

"Shit," I grumbled as I wrapped the broken glass in paper before tossing it.

"Dude, stop with the pissy attitude. We're all sick of it." Jared rolled his eyes at my outburst. "Just ask her out."

"Shut up." I glared at him and spent the rest of the afternoon working in silence, pretending I wasn't checking my phone at ten-minute intervals.

The sun was almost down when I got off the train and turned onto my street, ready to pass out from the long day of getting everything ready. Right as I reached my front entrance, I made an impulsive decision to keep walking, and I didn't stop for several blocks.

I felt like a stalker as I approached Al's house. She probably wasn't even home. She must have been busy the past two days, and that was why she hadn't been reaching out, I reasoned. Once outside I saw that there was a light on. Everything was illuminated in the living room in contrast to the evening sky. I saw Al slouched on the sofa and didn't even stop to think as I made a beeline for her front door, taking the steps two at a time.

I knocked three times and shoved my hands in my pockets, waiting for her to answer. Seconds later she was at the door in an all-gray sweats outfit. Her short hair was pulled back, and she looked shocked to see me.

"Dean? Hi, what are yo—"

"I was walking home and thought I'd stop by. Can I come in?" That was only a half lie.

She had barely stepped out of the way before I barreled past her. After a quick scan of the living room, it appeared that she was home alone.

Once inside I realized I had no idea what I was doing there or what to say.

"How was your day?" she asked hesitantly.

I was acting erratic, and I knew she could sense my weirdness. Realizing I was rocking back and forth, I forced my body to be still.

"It was fine." I tried my best to sound nonchalant. "How was yours?"

"It was okay, I guess. Just the typical routine of dealing with my work nemesis." Al smiled, clearly hoping to lighten the mood.

My mouth refused to return her gesture, and my foot continued to tap again. Why the hell was I acting like this?

She waited for me to say something, and when I didn't, she continued to try and fill the awkward void that I was creating. "Yesterday was good too. Cam and I made dinner at the house while Sean and Nora had their first official date." Her eyes lit up as she started to gush. "I'm so happy for them. They can't stop smiling at each other. It's pretty cute."

"Is that what this is about?" I demanded.

Her eyebrows drew together in confusion. "What are you talking about?"

"Are you pissed at me because I said I didn't know if I wanted to date? This is what I get for trying to be honest with you?"

She narrowed her eyes and shook her head slowly at me. "I'm so confused."

"I've hardly heard from you since you left Sunday morning. What's that about?" I sounded like an oaf, but I didn't care.

Her mouth hung open as she looked at me as if I had grown a second head. "I thought we were keeping this casual."

"Not *this* casual." I threw up my hands in frustration and looked at her exasperatedly. "I don't want this."

Al snorted and turned away from me. Taking a few steps back, she perched on the edge of the couch. "Then what *do* you want?" She looked at me expectantly, almost irritated.

Seeing her sudden change of demeanor made me hesitate. In the few weeks that I'd known her, I'd never seen her throw one annoyed glance in my direction. Now I was feeling a little chilly from her icy glare.

She threw her hands up and crossed her arms. "This is unbelievable," she huffed. "All I've done since I've met you is try to communicate with you in a way that doesn't make you bolt. I'm so sick of overthinking everything. You know why I didn't text you back?" Her question is clearly rhetorical. "Because I thought that would make me too available and then you'd be done with me. So I'm sick of trying to guess what it is you want. You're going to have to spell it out for me."

Her bottom lip quivered when she was done, and I knew that it took a lot out of her to confront me like that. Feeling like a jackass, I took two long strides toward her and took a seat next to her on the couch. Taking her chin in my hand, I tilted it up so that she would be forced to meet my gaze.

"I *want* you to text me back. I *want* to talk to you." *Because I haven't been able to open up like this with anyone,* I think but don't say out loud. "And I want you to want to hang out with me again because Saturday night was the best freaking night I've had since...since I don't even know when."

A tiny tremor at the corner of Al's mouth made it clear that she was holding back a smile. "That doesn't sound that casual." She lost control, and her lips curved upward.

The tightness in my chest finally loosened at the sight of her smile. I grabbed her forearms and pulled her toward me before wrapping my arms around her and kissing the top of her head.

"I didn't like not hearing from you. I'm sorry I suck at this, but I need you to know I'm trying." I pulled away from the embrace and held on to her arms, pressing my forehead against hers. "I want us both to try, okay?"

An adorable crease formed on her forehead as her eyes darted, searching mine for something. "So...so you *do* want to date?" Her voice was barely above a whisper.

The back of my neck immediately broke out in a sweat at the mention of the word. I took a deep sigh before continuing. The next words I spoke needed to be careful. "Look, I'm sorry. I don't know how to be in a relationship." Why was I saying this? I hadn't even thought about anyone else since she entered the picture. Still, something about the thought of her being my girlfriend made my chest hurt. This was already stepping way outside my comfort zone. "Let's forget about all these stupid labels and just see where this goes."

The hint of disappointment Al tried to hide didn't go unnoticed by me. I knew she deserved better than what I was offering her, but selfishly I didn't care. Right now, it felt like she was mine, and that feeling alone made my heart pump with adrenaline. I leaned forward and captured her lips with mine. I kissed her like I was afraid it could have been the last time. My mouth moved eagerly over hers, and I knew I had her when she tangled her fingers in my hair.

After a few minutes of making out, I pulled away and looked at her. "Will you come to our soft opening?"

"Um, isn't that for, like, friends and family and important people?"

I chuckled. "Yes. And you're important to me. I want you there."

"Then I'll be there." She beamed at me.

"This is beautiful."

"A little bit of an upgrade from the diner, huh?" I took in Al's excited face and was glad I had invited her here.

We were sitting across from each other at a small high-top table. The skyline of Chicago twinkled outside the floor-to-ceiling windows. The restaurant I had picked was crowded but still had an intimate feel to it. It also wasn't overly fancy. I figured Al wouldn't be into all that. Normally, I took dates to Luna, but she had already been there a few times and I wanted tonight to feel different. I was embarrassed to admit how much thought I had put into this date.

After Saturday night and our talk on Monday, I was completely hooked. Even though I was insanely swamped with getting the restaurant ready, I still found time to see her three times this week, including tonight. With all the excuses I'd made about being too busy for anything serious, it turned out that it wasn't that hard to find time for someone when you wanted to.

On Tuesday, she had come over late, and I made her a quick dinner, which she was adorably grateful for. I would have thought after working all day that hanging out would be exhausting, but Al being at my house felt comfortable. It felt right.

Last night, we even went on a double date with Tiff and Eric to watch the new horror movie I had been dying to see. Al agreed to it even though it was apparent pretty early on that she hated horror movies. She was an anxious wreck and spent the majority of the film watching it from behind my arm. It was ridiculously endearing.

"What are you thinking about?"

Her soft voice brought me back to the present.

"Just about how much of a wuss you are with scary movies."

"Hey," she exclaimed, and threw her napkin at me.

I chuckled and caught it easily. "No, but for real...I was thinking about how much fun I've been having with you. It's so easy being with you."

"It's easy being with you too." Her cheeks went slightly pink at my compliment, and a smile tugged at her lips. "Thanks again for picking this place. I love it."

"Well, I wanted to take you on a real date. Your first one, right?"

She rolled her eyes. "I've been on dates before...just not this nice."

"I disagree. You told me at the diner that you had never been taken out to dinner before."

She paused and gave me a funny look. "You remember that?"

I shrugged. "I remember everything you say."

"Well, I guess this is technically my first time."

"I'm honored to be your first."

"Can I have my napkin back so I can throw it at you again?"

Laughing, I reached across the table and grabbed her hand.

If she's so easy to be with, why do I still feel panicky at the thought of committing to her?

Brushing off my intrusive thought, I resumed staring out the window, taking comfort in our silence.

TWENTY-SEVEN
AL

"I'm glad we're finally hanging out. You two are freaking annoying with your couple bubbles. This honeymoon phase isn't going to last forever, you know?" Cam huffed at me as he squinted back and forth from his canvas to the demonstration one in the center of the room. "I don't understand how to do the water reflection. Mine looks like a swirl of shit."

He had a point. His colors blended together in a way that did not at all resemble the skyline of Chicago that we had been tasked to paint. It was Saturday night, and Nora had enlisted Cam and me to join one of those group classes that involved painting and drinking wine. Instructing was Nora's latest side job.

As if sensing Cam's frustration, Nora worked her way around the room until she was standing behind us.

"How are we doing over here?" she inquired, pretending like we were random members of the class. She leaned into Cam's canvas. "Really love the abstract approach you're taking here."

He glared at her. "Well, if someone hadn't gone so fast

during the demonstration portion, maybe I would have had the chance to get it right."

Nora rolled her eyes. "Art is about freedom of expression. You're taking this too seriously."

"Hey, I paid thirty-five dollars to paint this freaking canvas, and I want to end up with something that doesn't make me ill to look at."

Laughing, I looked over at him with feigned sympathy. "I like it, Cam. I'd be happy to hang it in the house."

"Al is right. Both of these beauties will be mounted for everyone to see. You should be proud."

"The only place I'm hanging this is above the toilet," Cam muttered.

"Excuse me, I have a question," an older woman called across the room.

"Be right there," Nora singsonged.

"I give up." Cam dropped his brush and picked up his wineglass, turning his full attention toward me. "So, what's the latest on you and Dean? You've certainly been spending a lot of time with him lately."

"It's nothing. We're hanging out."

Cam shoved my shoulder lightly. "Stop with the coyness. My dating life is pathetically nonexistent right now, and Nora and Sean are lovely, but, let's be honest, boring with a capital *B*. I need you to spill your guts so I can live vicariously through you."

Smiling, I continued painting highlights onto my skyscrapers. Things with Dean had been going shockingly well. Even though he had said that what we were doing was not dating, it sure felt like it was. When we were out with Tiff and Eric the other night, he held my hand in front of them, and when Tiff had gushed about how excited she was that we were together, he had kissed the top of my head instead of trying to correct her.

Then yesterday after a fantastic date that he had planned, I spent the night. There was a lot of making out and touching, but we hadn't had sex yet. When I told him I thought I was ready, he crushed me against his chest and kissed me intensely.

Almost, he had responded. Then he told me he wanted to take me somewhere special on Sunday and that he had something he wanted to ask me.

I glanced over to see Cam still staring at me, waiting for a response.

"I don't want to jinx it, but I think he might ask me to be his girlfriend tomorrow."

"Already?" Cam exclaimed so loudly that every head turned in our direction.

"Is everything okay over there, sir?" Nora asked through a gritted smile.

"Oh yes, I just can't believe this amazing class is *already* almost over." Cam's over-the-top polite response oozed sarcasm.

Nora shook her head but bit back a grin as she continued through the next part of the demonstration. Cam's attention returned to me as he awaited my response.

"So last night—and all week really—he's been acting very boyfriend-y. And then he tells me that he has something important he wants to ask me. I don't want to get my hopes up, but he's hitting me over the head with every sign possible."

"Oh my God, he's totally going to ask you. I can't believe it. You tamed him."

"Dean hardly needed taming. That's ridiculous," I insisted, feeling defensive of him. "He just has a complicated past. It's hard for him to open up."

"Well, kudos to you, girl. He's certainly opening up to you."

Cam wiggled his eyebrows. "Speaking of being open, how's the sex?"

"Cam, stop. We haven't even had sex yet."

Everything we *had* done so far had been amazing. Like, I-have-an-orgasm-from-him-barely-touching-me amazing. But I wasn't about to tell Cam all that.

"What are you waiting for?" he whisper-yelled.

I grinned at him. "I think tomorrow night might be the night."

We both squealed.

"Can you two please keep it down? The class is almost over," Nora reprimanded us from the front.

"I'm sorry," I mouthed to her.

"Tell me later," she mouthed back, and winked.

The cool breeze blew my hair away from my face as I leaned against the open car window. It was starting to feel like fall, and I couldn't have felt cozier in my oversized oatmeal sweater and light-wash jeans. Dean squeezed my other hand, which was resting on the center console with his own.

"This is perfect," I murmured.

The skin around his eyes crinkled as he half smiled, probably my favorite of his mannerisms. "We aren't even there yet."

"Doesn't matter. It's already perfect."

We had been driving for about forty-five minutes. I knew we were headed south, but he hadn't told me where we were going yet. Dean had been pretty quiet since we met up this afternoon, and I couldn't help but feel like maybe he was a little nervous. Suddenly, I had the urge to comfort him, so I leaned toward him and brought his hand to my mouth, kissing his fingertips.

He gifted me with his famous half smile again.

A few minutes later, Dean pulled up to the entrance of a state park and paid the parking fee. After we parked, he rushed around to my side of the van to open my door and help me down. Before we set off walking, he grabbed me around the waist and pulled me in for a lingering kiss. I felt like I was on cloud nine.

He led me to a wooden staircase that led to a bridge through a forested area. The forested area opened up to reveal a breathtaking view of endless white sand with a backdrop of Lake Michigan.

"It's beautiful," I exclaimed. "I had no idea this was so close to the city."

"It gets pretty crowded in the summer, but I love to come here once the temperature drops a little."

We took our shoes off and started walking down the sand dune, toward the water. I snuck a glance at Dean, who was one pace behind me.

Without warning, I took off, sprinting down the hill. "Race you!" I screamed behind me.

"No fair!" Dean shouted. I snuck a glance behind me to see that his long legs were gaining on me.

Laughing, I picked up my pace. I was just feet from the water when I felt strong arms wrap around my waist and my feet started to lift off the ground.

"Dean, stop it." I could barely get the words out through my laughter.

He tumbled to the ground, causing me to land on top of him before he rolled over, pinning me underneath him. A dark curl hung in his face as he stared down at me. His laugh gave way to breathlessness as he tried to regain his composure.

"Cheater," he accused me.

"Hey, you tackled me."

"You got a head start."

"Your legs are a foot longer than mine. I needed it."

"Aren't we the scrappy one?" Dean tickled my rib cage with one hand, and I screeched in surprise.

"Stop that."

"Stop what?" Dean's green eyes feigned puppy-dog innocence.

"This," I said, tickling him in the same spot that he got me. His body jerked away from my touch before he attacked the other side of my torso with tickles.

I squealed as my body writhed beneath him. "Truce!" I yelled.

We were both laughing hysterically when he finally rolled off me.

Dean sat up and pulled me toward him so that my back was resting on his chest. I settled into his warm torso, and he engulfed me with his strong arms. He absentmindedly started to trace circles on my upper arm.

"It's so peaceful here right now." We both looked off into the vast water. Neither of us spoke for a while, and I couldn't remember a time I had felt this content. Eventually, Dean's deep voice broke our trance.

"My mom took me here once."

My breath hitched at the mention of his late mother.

"It was after she got sick. One day she showed up at my school and pulled me out of class. We drove for hours and wound up here."

His words sounded tight, almost as if he was clenching his jaw.

"We just sat here and stared at the water. We didn't talk much. But something felt lighter about that day, so far away from my father. That moment made me feel like she wished she could have been better for me. Made me feel like she wished she weren't leaving me. It took me a while to come back here after she died, but once I did, I started coming every year around the same time. It's nice to have at least one memory of her that isn't tarnished by him."

Tears pricked at the back of my eyes, and I didn't say anything for a few minutes.

"Thanks for telling me," I finally murmured.

He wrapped his arms around my shoulders and held me tight. I inhaled his scent and sniffled a little. Dean sat up and grabbed my chin, forcing my face into his eyeline.

"Are you crying?" he demanded.

"No," I lied.

He kissed me and stroked my cheek with his thumb.

"I didn't mean to make you cry."

I shrugged. "It just hurts to think about you being hurt."

His eyebrows drew together, and his eyes darkened a little as he averted his gaze back to the water.

"I *really* like you," Dean finally said, so quietly it felt like maybe I imagined it.

We spent the next hour walking up and down the shoreline, Dean occasionally stopping to skip any flat stones we came across. He attempted to teach me, but all of mine fell as soon as they hit the clear water. It was starting to get dark when Dean finally mentioned heading back. I wanted to protest. Going back to the city right now felt like it would break this magical spell we were under.

The car was about a half mile back. He held my hand, and I felt so grateful that he brought me here. I bit the inside of my cheek, not forgetting that he hadn't mentioned anything about the question he said he'd wanted to ask me. Taking a deep breath in, I decided I couldn't let it go.

"So, um, didn't you say you had a question you wanted to ask me?"

Dean stopped and turned so that he was facing me. He scratched the back of his neck and looked down at me before averting his eyes to the sand beneath our feet. Was he nervous? My heart was pounding. *This was it.*

"Would you maybe..."

I nodded, trying to appear calm but freaking out on the inside.

"Want to..."

Yes.

"Be my date to Eric and Tiff's wedding?"

His eyes returned to mine, and his lip turned up in a shy smile.

My chest deflated a bit before taking in that this was still a great milestone.

"Of course." He leaned down to kiss me, and I wrapped my arms around his strong torso.

My eyes drooped closed as I drifted in and out of consciousness, Dean's arm providing the perfect pillow.

"Al, wake up." He jerked me gently.

"Mmm," I responded, pretending to still be asleep.

"This is the best part."

I cracked an eye open to take in the movie he had insisted on putting on. It was an action movie, not my favorite. Our day had been so amazing, though, that I accepted his pick without a debate.

"How is this car chase better than the first fifty?"

He looked at me bewildered. "I know you are not shitting on this movie."

My eyes grew wide as I feigned innocence. "I love this movie."

"Very convincing." He rolled his eyes and smirked down at me.

Without warning, his eyes grew dark, and I felt hot under his gaze. I shifted up so that I was in more of a sitting position.

"I-I'm really glad you came with me today." His voice was husky, causing me to blink nervously.

The sudden change in his demeanor did not go unnoticed by me. This whole week we had been making out and doing a lot of fun stuff, but one of us always pumped the brakes before we went too far. Dean had told me numerous times that he was glad we were taking things slow.

After today, though, things between us felt different. Heavier. I wanted him before, but now the need felt a lot stronger. More intense. There was a tingly sensation between my legs that begged for his touch.

Without thinking too much about it, I leaned in and pressed my lips to his. Dean returned my kiss passionately. His tongue slipped into my mouth, and his hands held on to my cheeks, holding me there.

I sat up even more and lifted one leg so that it fell to the other side of his body, straddling him. He broke the kiss for a moment to look up at me with surprise, but I immediately crushed my mouth back onto his. As the kiss deepened, I slowly started to grind against him, feeling his need for me almost immediately. I moaned as the sensation between my legs started to build.

"Fuck, I want you," Dean said against my mouth.

"Bedroom," I commanded.

He broke away again, this time holding my face a few inches away from his so I couldn't move. "Al, are you sure?"

I nodded, knowing my eyes held just as much lust as his did.

"Because I meant it when I said we can take things slow."

"I know."

"We don't have to do anything you're not ready for."

"I know."

"And I wo—"

I forcibly removed his hands from my face and stopped his rant with my lips. "Dean, shut up."

"Okay." He bit the bottom of my lip before grabbing my ass in his two large hands. He stood up, and I wrapped my legs around him as he walked us toward the bedroom. Once there, he threw us onto the bed, making sure not to let any of his weight land on top of me.

He took off my shirt as I fumbled with the zipper of his jeans. In two seconds, we were both naked except for our underwear, and I eagerly pulled his chest against mine, needing to feel his skin against my bare breasts.

"Fuck, I want you so bad."

"Then take me," I murmured.

He continued to kiss every inch of my body until I was begging for him. When he finally slid inside me, I almost burst, completely undone from the pleasure.

Later, when he was lying next to me, still naked, playing with my hair, I knew I had fallen—hard. I hoped everything I thought he was feeling was real because there was no way I could continue to pretend that what I was feeling was casual.

TWENTY-EIGHT
DEAN

The renovations at Luna Two were finally complete, and not a moment too soon, with the impending opening being this weekend. Today Eric and I supervised the new staff training. Pretty much all that was left to do were some minor finishing touches.

"We did it, man." Eric smacked me on the back.

"Let's never try to open a restaurant in less than two months again."

"I don't know. I think we might have discovered our special talent," Eric joked. "Maybe we can take this business model to investors."

"Thanks, but I'm not a masochist."

Eric snorted. "Sorry to break this to you, Dean, but you definitely are."

My mouth fell open as I looked at him appalled. We were interrupted by Tiff and Jared coming through the front door, holding a bottle of champagne.

"Who's ready to celebrate?" Tiff came up to Eric and gave him a loud smack on the lips before giving me a polite kiss on the cheek.

"Isn't it a little early for that?" I was a little superstitious, and celebrating a restaurant before opening day didn't seem right to me.

"You should celebrate all the wins, big and small. If you wait until the end to celebrate, you could be waiting forever."

"How insightful, Jared." Eric grabbed us all glasses from behind the bar. "Is your new philosophical brain Janelle's influence?"

Jared beamed as he gushed about his new girlfriend. I was surprised to admit that I was incredibly happy for him. If you had told me one month ago that I would be excited that my best friend and long-time fellow singleton had a girlfriend, I would have said you were crazy.

My thoughts drifted to Al. We had spent the most amazing night together a few days ago, and I hadn't been able to stop thinking about her. Unfortunately, the long hours readying Luna Two had kept me from her this week, but I made sure she knew *exactly* how much I missed her via some especially dirty text messages.

"What about you and Al?"

I returned my attention to Tiff and the conversation I had been zoning out on.

"Sorry, what did you ask?"

"Are you going to make things official with Al?" she asked me.

I shrugged, immediately putting my guard up.

Tiff crossed her arms over her chest, not bothering to hide her irritation with me. "I don't get you. You treat her like she's your girlfriend. I haven't seen you with any other women in weeks. You invited her to our wedding. What are you so scared of? You're basically already in a relationship, and you don't even realize it."

"She's got a point there, Dean." Eric wiggled his eyebrows at me.

I knew they both had the best of intentions, but I already felt my emotions shutting down because of this interrogation. "It's none of your business."

Tiff groaned at my lame response. "Whatever, you're right. As long as *you* know that Al isn't going to wait around forever."

"What's that supposed to mean?"

"Just that if you don't ask her soon, someone else will. I know a few nice guys I would love to set her up with."

My nostrils flared as I glared down at her. "Don't you dare," I growled.

She snorted at my obvious sign of hostility. "Don't worry, she's too hung up on you." Tiff playfully batted my arm. "Don't mess this up, okay? You two are great together."

Tiff's words from earlier were playing in my head on repeat. *If you don't ask her soon, someone else will.*

I paced the length of my living room a few times, mulling over my next move. Al had just gotten off of work and was on her way here.

I knew three things for certain.

1. I had never felt for anyone the way I felt for Al.
2. The thought of commitment nauseated me.
3. There was absolutely no way in hell I was letting her go.

Considering those three things made my next move a lot clearer. I knew what I had to do. I had finally met someone that made the fear of losing her way worse than my fear of a relationship.

My phone rang, and I hurried to answer it, figuring it would be Al letting me know her ETA.

But the voice on the other end of the line immediately made the hair on the back of my neck bristle and my jaw tense.

TWENTY-NINE
AL

"Hey, where are you?" Dean's voice sounded tense and rushed.

"I just left work. I should be there in twenty minutes."

"Good, you aren't almost here. Listen, something has come up. I have to go back home, so I'll be gone for a day or two."

My breath hitched. Back home? From what Dean had told me, "home" wasn't exactly a place that he held dear. No wonder his mood seemed off.

"Is everything all right?"

"Yep," he responded in a clipped tone.

I gulped. "Will your father be the—"

"I have to go. I'll try to call you when I get a chance."

The phone went dead, and I stopped in my tracks. Dean had never been so short with me. I guess I could give him a pass, since he sounded like he was dealing with something shitty, but still, he could have at least given me a two-sentence explanation.

Pushing the crappy call to the back of my mind, I caught my usual train home.

Hours later I was almost happy that Dean had to cancel on me tonight. Sean, Nora, Cam, and I were all home at the same time, which hadn't happened in almost a week. We had all settled in to watch the latest romantic comedy that had just come out. Sean was outnumbered once again.

Cam and I sat on the floor eating popcorn, while on the couch, Nora rested her head on Sean's shoulder. It was nice to see them being so comfortable around each other. I hated it when Nora felt like she couldn't have the relationship she wanted because we all lived together.

Despite the evening being cozy and perfect, I couldn't help but worry about Dean. He did not sound like his head was in a good place earlier. I had texted him a few times to try to make sure he was okay but had yet to hear anything back from him.

After the movie, we all decided to hit the sack early. I decided to message Dean one more time before falling asleep.

Al: Hey, about to go to bed but just wanted to let you know I'm thinking about you. Hope everything is okay.

A blank spreadsheet stared back at me from my computer, mocking me. I couldn't focus at all on work, so instead I reread the message Dean had sent me late last night. The only text message, mind you.

Dean: I told you that everything is fine and I'll talk to you when I get a chance. Please stop bombarding me with messages.

The audacity of him to send me that message. He didn't give me any explanation for bailing on our plans, hasn't spoken to me at all since, and had the nerve to ask me to "stop bombarding" him when all I had done was send three texts asking if he was okay.

My blood was boiling. This was not how I was envisioning things going between us after our magical evening together. I was stupid enough to think he was going to ask me to be his girlfriend.

"Hey, Al, got a sec?" Trent appeared out of nowhere, leaning against my cubicle. He was wearing a sweater vest underneath a quarter-zip sweatshirt despite it still being seventy degrees inside our office.

"What's up?"

"I wanted to check on that report I asked about yesterday. Is it almost done? I was kind of expecting you'd get it to me first thing this morning."

"The one you mentioned on my way out the door yesterday?" I asked through gritted teeth. "I'm working on it, and considering that it's only"—I checked the time on my computer—"just after ten, I'm still going to need a few more hours to finish it."

Trent whistled. "Okay, I'll tell Shelley. Try and hurry it along though."

I fought the urge to flip him off as he walked away. While my love life had been on the incline—until recently—my work life had taken a nosedive. Trent's attempt to micromanage me had been making me miserable. I had done some easy marketing work for one of Nora's artist friends last week, and I had another inquiry from someone she referred to me. My résumé had also been updated and sent out to every position I was qualified for, and some that I wasn't. I was sick of waiting around for this job to get better. I needed to be somewhere that gave me an ounce of respect.

Picking up a little extra cash from the freelance gig had been nice, but I knew I had to wait for a real job and benefits before I put my notice in here. I crossed my fingers that I'd hear back soon about an interview.

Later that evening I was lounging with my roommates again. We were arguing over what to watch. Cam wanted to watch the newest terrible reality dating show, and the rest of us were trying to veto him.

"Why are you all even here anyway?" Cam crossed his arms over his chest after losing the battle. "Shouldn't you all be on dates?"

"Just because we're dating now doesn't mean we don't want to hang out with you." Sean smirked at Cam.

"I'm *so* lucky. Thank you for taking pity on poor single Cam." He rolled his eyes before turning on me. "What about you? I'm surprised you haven't been at Dean's the past few nights."

"Oh, h-he's been busy." I stumbled over my words. Normally, I might vent to my roommates about my worries that Dean might be pulling away. But bringing up his issues with his home life seemed like a betrayal of trust.

Besides, the more I stewed about his last message, the more forgiving I felt. Yes, he was being short with me and not leaning on me, but we had just started getting more serious, and I knew that this was a touchy topic for him. I was sure that things would be back to normal when he got home and we could talk about it.

THIRTY
DEAN

The bags underneath my eyes were dark from the lack of sleep I got last night. The motel bed was lumpy, and I had tossed and turned all night. The visceral reaction to seeing my father again after all these years had been one of disgust.

I had hardly seen my father since I moved out at eighteen. The few times I had spoken to him had only brought me misery, so a while back, I vowed to cut off all ties.

That changed when he called and told me he was moving. That he was planning on throwing anything that had belonged to my mother or me away. If I wanted any of it, I had better get down there immediately.

Seeing him again confirmed one thing—the bastard hadn't changed at all. When I finally walked through the threshold of the home that had been a living hell for me, I was greeted with silence and the stench of cigarettes. I thought back to the previous day, and the few words my father had deigned to speak to me played on repeat in my head.

"I can't believe your sorry ass came just to pick up a bunch of trash." Those were the first words he had said to me in person after five years.

He looked terrible, even worse than I remembered. His beer gut had doubled in size, and the remaining teeth he had left looked to be badly stained. The consequences of a lifelong addiction to alcohol and cigarettes.

"I'll be out of here shortly."

Stepping into my childhood bedroom felt like stepping through a time portal. Although the room had changed, the painful memories still lingered. Opening the closet, I found boxes of my old things littered on the floor.

"Not so fast." My father ambled into the room after me. "You could help me move my stuff into the truck tomorrow. It's the least you can fucking do."

I froze, glaring at him. "Oh, I'm sorry, have I not been there for *you*? I wonder who I could have learned that from."

"Not this crap again. I gave you a house over your head all those years, you little prick. You and your mother were always so fucking ungrateful."

Taking a deep breath, I bit my tongue. The last thing I wanted to do was engage with him. All of my experience had proved to me that he wasn't worth it.

"I'll just grab some things and be on my way."

"Hold your horses. I asked you to help me tomorrow. Are you deaf?"

Tomorrow was Friday, the day of our soft opening.

"I can't," I barked. "My new restaurant is opening, and I have to be there."

I should have known better than to share any details about my life with him, but part of me wanted to rub my success in his face. Show him that I made something of myself despite him tearing me down every chance he got.

"*Your* new restaurant, huh? Must be easy to be you when

your rich little friends just hand you everything in life. What a fucking joke. Back in my day, we knew the value of hard work and making a living."

His words were like a smack in the face, reminding me why I should never disclose anything to him. He just used it as ammunition to make me feel worthless. Putting my head down, I tried to tune him out and started packing the boxes I had brought with photographs and some old trinkets that had belonged to my mother.

Our brief phone call informed me that he was moving to Arizona for "work." I didn't bother asking him any follow-up questions. The additional miles between us were welcome, and I was content to go back to pretending he didn't exist. Until Al, I hadn't spoken of my father in years.

The thought of Al immediately ripped me from my thoughts about yesterday and back to the present. For some reason, I had been avoiding her messages. The fact that she was concerned about me enough to check in multiple times made me feel irrationally irritated. I was fine. I had been dealing with this my entire life. I didn't need her.

Taking a deep breath, I fought off my inner rage and the hostility I was feeling. I knew that none of this was really about Al. I finished throwing my toiletries and a few pieces of clothing into my backpack. The car was already packed and ready to go. Checking my watch, I cursed at the time. It was a three-hour drive back to the city, and I had to head out now to make it back in time to help with the opening. Grabbing my phone, I saw that Al had sent me one message since I had blown her off last night.

Al: Do you still want me to come tonight?

THIRTY-ONE

AL

Nervously, I checked my reflection in the mirror for the hundredth time that evening. Dean had assured me that it was casual, but I didn't want to look too underdressed. I tugged at the hem of the patterned black dress I was wearing. I paired it with an oversized blazer that Nora and I had recently thrifted. Looking down at my feet, I debated changing out of my combat boots but convinced myself that the rest of the outfit dressed them up enough.

Grabbing my phone, I reread the last texts that Dean had sent me.

Al: Do you still want me to come tonight?

Dean: Yes, but I'll have to meet you there. Driving back this morning and then I'll head straight there.

Al: Excited to see you. :)

Dean: Me too.

His words weren't exactly a declaration of love, but he still said he wanted me there. I refused to do what I always did and read too much into this. He was having a hard time with some things emotionally, and I needed to be there for him.

Luna Two was one train stop away, so I decided to walk it and clear my head. Tiff had texted me earlier saying that she would meet me outside so that we could go in together. Eric had some errands he needed to run beforehand, and she had to work late.

The evening air was brisk, which caused me to walk at a faster pace than normal. When I arrived outside the restaurant, there was already a small crowd forming at the front of the brick building.

"Al, over here." Tiff looked stunning in a mid-length satin dress that complimented her blonde hair perfectly. We embraced in a quick hug that didn't feel forced at all. "I'm so glad you're here. I don't know anyone. Oh my God, I love your outfit."

"Thanks." I smiled at her. "Are Eric and Dean here yet?"

"I'm sure they're inside schmoozing with all of the arrivals. Let's head in."

The inside was beautifully decorated, not that the building needed much help. The walls were all original brick, and wood beams drew your eyes up to the tall ceilings. Some of the tables were moved out of the way so there was more of a gathering area by the shiny oak bar. The vibrant green on the walls made me flash back to when I had run into Dean at that hardware store weeks ago. The thought made me smile.

Eric spotted us immediately and waved us over. Tiff leapt into his arms, and he gave her a big kiss on the mouth. I tried to imagine doing that with Dean.

"Hey, Al." I was surprised that he went in for a hug, but even more surprised to find that it didn't feel awkward.

"The place looks great," I told him.

Just then, Dean stepped around the crowd. He looked amazing in dark jeans, a tight gray T-shirt, and a well-fitted black utility jacket.

Before I could overthink the best way to greet him, he grabbed me around the waist and pulled me into a warm embrace. I inhaled his scent, relieved that my worrying had been for nothing.

"Missed you," he whispered, kissing the top of my head.

I smiled up at him. His eyes were dark, and the lines between his eyes were deep. He looked distracted and stressed out, but I was sure that had nothing to do with me.

"Missed you too."

Dean had been distant all night. After greeting me, he had been racing off in every direction. He had even spent an hour mingling with investors, an activity I knew made him want to barf. I could have suffered through the networking with him if he'd let me. I would have loved to chalk up his lack of attention to the fact that it was his restaurant's opening and he was busy, but Eric had barely left Tiff's side all evening.

A waiter came by with a plate of appetizers, and I gobbled some up while scanning the crowd for Dean's floppy head of hair. I spotted him in the corner talking to Jared and Janelle and took off to say hi before he could evade me again.

Jared greeted me with a grin and a side hug.

"Isn't this fantastic?" Janelle exclaimed.

"Definitely," I replied. I smiled up at Dean, but he didn't

make eye contact with me. "Dean, do you want to grab a drin—"

"I should go check on the kitchen, excuse me." He bolted away from the group without giving me a second look.

I rubbed my hands together, feeling uncomfortable. Jared and Janelle stared at me in confusion, so I attempted to force a smile. It seemed clear at this point that Dean was avoiding me on purpose.

The rest of the evening flew by in a blur. Tiff thankfully found me huddled in a corner alone and took pity on me. We chatted for a long time, and she graciously did not bring up Dean's apathetic attitude toward me.

People were starting to filter out, and any buzz I was feeling from being invited tonight had worn off long ago. Why had he asked me to come if he was planning to ignore me all night? I even double-checked this morning to make sure he still wanted me here. I would have done anything to avoid this feeling of embarrassment.

It felt like a lifetime had passed since that magical evening on the beach, not a few days. With the way Dean was avoiding me, any outsider would think I was some obsessed ex and not the girl he was seeing.

Feeling dejected, I decided to head home. Nothing about this night felt salvageable. Maybe it was stupid, but I still held hope that Dean would make it up to me. After all, he did have an insanely stressful week.

Halfway to the door, Tiff called my name from the bar. "Al, get over here."

Tiff, Todd, and Dean were all standing by the bar. Eric appeared to be pouring celebratory glasses of champagne.

The exit was calling my name, but I didn't want to seem rude. Reluctantly, I plastered on one more smile for the evening and took the spot next to Dean.

"Tonight was great, but there are a few things I noticed I want to change before the grand opening tomorrow." Todd was obnoxiously loud.

Tiff rolled her eyes and looked up at Eric. "Tonight was perfect. The food was to die for, the drinks were amazing, and the staff was on top of everything."

"You guys should be proud of yourselves." I smiled up at Dean.

He rolled his eyes and gave me a hard look. "There's still a lot to do," he muttered while swirling his drink.

His short response stung, and I looked down at my feet. I should have dropped it, but I was feeling especially defensive after enduring his cold shoulder all evening.

"I didn't say there wasn't. I just meant you've done so much already. The place is clearly a success. You should be proud of what you've done so far."

His laugh came out bitter. "You don't get it at all. We don't *know* if this place is a success yet. We won't know that for a while."

"Dean, why don't you back off?" Tiff was glaring at him.

"Uh-oh, is this some type of lover's quarrel?" Todd looked amusedly between Dean and me. "You better apologize to your girlfriend, Deanie boy."

"She's *not* my girlfriend," he snapped.

His outburst sent a dagger right through my chest. I know we hadn't had any type of conversation about that yet, but the way he said I didn't belong to him, like the idea repulsed him, stung. Shit, I could feel tears welling up behind my eyes.

"It's getting late. I should probably head out. Congrats again."

Tiff hugged me goodbye and whispered, "he's an ass."

Dean said nothing but set down his drink and moved behind me, making it clear that he was going to walk me out.

I took deep breaths through my nose on the way to the door, begging my tears to recede and to stay calm. Once outside I turned toward him, putting on a braver face than I felt.

"What the fuck was that about?" he demanded immediately.

My eyebrows shot up in surprise. *He* was upset with *me*? I was too shocked to say anything, so he continued.

"You're upset because I was busy tonight and because I didn't call you my girlfriend back there, so you're leaving. We've talked about this so many times. You know I'm not ready. It isn't cool the way you're constantly pressuring me. Obviously, what I'm offering you isn't good enough."

My mouth hung open. I felt too hurt to speak, but I tried to gather the buzzing thoughts floating around my head.

"I know you're busy, which is why I hung out with Tiff at the bar, but you barely said anything to me all night. And trust me, I know I'm not your girlfriend. You've made that crystal clear." My repressed anger was starting to bubble to the surface. How dare he be mad at me right now? "But you didn't have to act so repulsed by the idea in front of everyone."

He rolled his eyes and glared at me. It was hard to believe that just days ago I was getting lost in those same green eyes.

"You're being dramatic and oversensitive."

"Look." My eyes darted away and then back to him. I was feeling flustered, but I felt determined to have a real conversation with him. "Last week was amazing. Probably the best week of my life. I felt so connected to you. Sure, it hurt a little when you didn't talk to me these past few days. I know that things are bad with your dad, so I gave you space. But I wish you felt comfortable talking to me after everything we've shared with each other. And then tonight"—I gestured at him—"you acted like you barely knew me. It feels like you've taken a step back from this, but I'm still a few steps forward, standing here like an idiot that didn't get the memo."

Dean started fidgeting. I silently begged for him to reach out to me, but instead he dug his hands deep into his pockets.

"I don't think I can do this anymore." My heart fractured at his easy response. "I just don't have the same feelings that you have for me."

"Are you being serious right now?" My mind flashed back to the amazing last week we had. Everything that he shared with me, the way he acted like he couldn't get enough of me.

"I'm sorry, Al." His eyes had softened a bit, and now they looked almost regretful. "I've got to get back inside."

He made a move like maybe he was going to hug me goodbye but hesitated when he took in my knit brow and down-turned lips. He gave a little wave before leaving me outside —alone.

"He *what*?" Cam looked like he was ready to commit murder. "That jerk. I always knew I didn't like him."

"Why would he even invite you if he was going to treat you like that?" Nora handed me a tissue.

My eyes were puffy from crying all night. When I finally made it downstairs the next morning, I was greeted by all three of my roommates immediately demanding to know what had caused my current state of despair.

"I don't want to talk about it," I whimpered before blowing my nose.

"What an asshole," Sean muttered.

"It's my fault. Everyone warned me about him."

"It's not your fault," Nora said fiercely. "He totally led you on."

"He love-bombed you," Cam insisted. "How were you supposed to resist the whole 'Oh, Al, let me take you to this romantic spot that means *so* much to me because you're *so* special'?" He gagged for effect.

Despite my miserable mood, I smiled at Cam's dramatic reenactment. They were all hovering over me voicing their concern and sympathy when I felt an overwhelming sense of gratitude. Which of course caused me to burst into another bout of tears.

"Oh no, what is it now?" Nora sat down on the couch next to me. "Is Cam being too insensitive?"

"N-no," I choked out. "I'm j-just so happy I met you all."

Nora beamed at me before pulling me into an embrace.

"Shit, he did a number on you if you're getting all sentimental now," Cam said before joining our hug.

Sean stood there awkwardly before Nora pulled at his sleeve to come join us.

"Oh, I'm good." He tried to resist.

"C'mon, Sean. This is probably the only time Al is going to let us get a group hug in."

"As long as it's the last one," he mumbled before joining us. His awkwardness reminded me of when I first moved in, and my tears quickly turned to laughter.

Rain splattered against the tall windows. I surveyed the storm outside from the safety of the common area in my office. People had started filing in for the day, but I was too distracted to join them. There was a big presentation I should be preparing for, but I felt too numb to care.

Trent and Shelley shuffled into a nearby conference room, and both gave me a confused look. Sighing, I set my coffee cup in the sink and tailed behind them. Ready to get this morning over with.

I plopped into the seat closest to the door. Putting my elbows on the table, I rested my chin in both my hands and waited for the meeting to start. The air was so dense inside from the humidity of the rain. It felt like I could suffocate at any moment.

Trent eyed me and the seat next to him and mouthed, "What are you doing?" at me. I pretended not to notice.

"Okay, I guess I'll get us started." Trent shot daggers at me as he started clicking through a slide presentation that was being cast to the TV.

The presentation consisted of an A/B test I had set up to compare how well different marketing campaigns were performing. Since I had already seen all of this information before, I immediately started to zone out.

"Al, did you hear me? I asked if you can explain what's on this chart. Is it showing a strong correlation or not?" Trent's eyes were wide. With Shelley's attention on me, he threw up his hands in frustration.

"Like I told you earlier, Trent, it's not showing any correlation."

"Well, why don't you come up here with me and explain it to Shelley?"

"What's the point when you'll just take credit for everything?" I demanded, suddenly feeling more anger than apathy. "I did this entire analysis. I put together this slide deck. I wrote you the notes that you're now using to present. You didn't do any of this work."

Shelley raised her eyebrows and looked between the two of us. Trent held up his hands. "That's ridiculous. I managed this entire project."

"Really? That's interesting. Because I seem to recall you

not showing up at any of the meetings I scheduled for this project."

"Now you're just lying," Trent whined.

"Enough, you two." Shelley rose from her swivel chair, taking command of the room. "This attitude is very disappointing. We're all a team here." By the way she was glaring only in my direction, I knew who she was talking about. "I was waiting until the end of the quarter to do this, but now I think sooner might be better." She walked toward the front of the conference room before continuing. "Trent, you will be managing Al from now on."

My spine straightened, and I shot up in my chair. "Excuse me?"

"You heard me. Al, you're smart, but you don't take enough initiative here. Trent is a natural leader, and I'm confident you'll flourish under his watchful eye."

Trent beamed. "Wow, Shelley, thank you so much for the opportunit—"

"No," I cut him off.

"This isn't up for negotiation." Shelley started to gather her things.

"Look, the only thing I'm certain of is that since I've started this job, Trent has taken credit for all of my work and all of my ideas. Maybe I should have 'taken more initiative.'" I formed air quotes around the words. "But the initiative I should have taken was to tell Trent off a long time ago. I'm good at this job. No. I'm great at this job. And I'm sorry, but I can't work here under these circumstances."

"Are you quitting?" Trent looked panicked. "You can't do this to me."

"Sorry, Trent." I feigned sympathy. "I'm sure you'll find someone else to take advantage of."

"Al, why don't we go into my office and talk?" Shelley was trying to keep the anger out of her voice.

"There's nothing to talk about. Shelley, I appreciate the opportunity to work here, and I'm sorry for not giving more notice. I've learned a lot, but I can't stay. Frankly, I'm miserable here, and I need to prioritize my mental health."

With that, I spun out of the room and went to my desk. Adrenaline was pumping through my veins. That felt *amazing*. Not sure if security was going to show up at any minute to escort me out, I rushed to pack my backpack. Thankfully, I didn't believe in bringing personal items to the office, so I was done in ten seconds.

An HR representative flagged me down on my way to the elevator, asking me to sign a few standard legal items. Once the elevator doors closed, it felt like a hundred-pound weight had been lifted off my chest. I heard laughter coming from somewhere, and then realized it was me when I caught my reflection in the elevator mirror. Who would have thought that having no stable source of income and no idea what I was going to do could make me feel so alive?

I skipped out of the building and into the pouring rain. Roaming the almost empty sidewalks when I would have normally been stuck at my desk was thrilling. The city was dark and gloomy, but to me, it looked beautiful.

"I can't believe you quit. Tell me again, every word." Jess sipped her coffee as she sat across from me in an overstuffed armchair.

The cafe was small and cozy, a great escape from the storm outside. I wrung out my hair, but it was still soaking wet. I was sure I looked like a mess. After I left work, I wandered downtown for over an hour. I couldn't stop moving. Finally, I texted Jess to see if she could sneak away and meet me.

"I feel amazing," I said after recounting the story. "I thought I would feel more scared—or nervous—but I don't. This job was holding me back in so many ways."

"I guess, but what are you going to do for money now?"

A question like that would have made me anxious a few weeks ago.

"Well, I already applied to a few positions, and I have a decent amount of savings. Plus, I've been doing a few freelance jobs."

Jess pursed her lips and remained silent. Desperately wanting to avoid hearing her opinion on my financial situation, I diverted the subject to Tom. She immediately lit up. The two of them had discussed getting engaged in the next year. As she rambled on about her love life, I felt a little pang, realizing mine was now nonexistent.

"What about you and Dean?" she asked as if reading my thoughts. "Last I heard, you thought it might be getting serious."

I sipped my coffee before responding. "Unfortunately, my relationship radar is still broken. We haven't spoken in a few days." I gave her a boiled-down version of the events, not wanting to rehash every single detail.

She nodded, her eyebrows knitting together with concern. I braced myself for the "I told you so."

"Well, I'm not surprised. This is exactly what I told you would happen. You can be so naive when it comes to guys."

Why did it feel like every time we spoke, she was putting me down in some way? The warm air started to feel suffocating instead of comfortable.

"He completely led me on."

"Oh, come on," she scoffed. "Everyone told you what he was like. You can't ignore all of the signs and then cry about it when he dumps you."

"You don't even know him."

"And you did?"

"Better than you. And don't tell me I ignored the signs. You weren't there. He was giving me every sign possible that he was interested."

"Whatever you say," she muttered into her mug.

"I'm so sick of this."

She snapped back into sympathy mode like a trained actor. "Don't worry, honey. You'll meet a guy someday. Maybe you should take my advice next time."

"No, not that. I'm sick of *you*."

Her mug clattered to the table as she looked at me wide-eyed, mouth agape.

"Excuse m—"

"You treat me like a child. Like I'm your dumb little friend that you need to take care of. 'Poor Al, tagging along again.' 'Poor Al, can't do anything without me.' I'm sick of it." I jolted out of my seat. "It's my fault for blindly following you all these years. You pretend like you're my best friend, but you only like me because you know I'll do whatever you say and follow you around like some lost puppy. When anything good happens to me, it's like you make it your mission to downplay it." I started to stalk off but then turned around. "I don't need your pity. I don't need your opinions. And I don't need this one-sided friendship anymore."

I left without giving her a chance to speak.

My heart didn't stop racing the whole train ride home. Part of me felt like I was too harsh with Jess. A lot was going on in my life, and maybe I took too much of it out on her. The other, larger, part of me knew there was truth in my outburst.

It occurred to me that I had quit my job and my best friend, all before lunch. I waited for the panic to set in, but all I felt was freedom and relief.

THIRTY-TWO
DEAN

The storm continued to rage outside as I sat in the comfort of my condo. My couch had a permanent indentation from all the time I had spent on it this past week. It was Saturday night, and I knew I should be at Luna Two right now. We had been crazy packed since the opening, and it was all-hands-on-deck. Even though I knew I was letting Eric down, I just couldn't get myself to get up.

It wasn't like me to bail on commitments, but I just felt so fucking numb. The opening should have felt like this amazing triumph. Thirty years old and co-owner of two restaurants in Chicago. Why didn't I care?

There was a banging at the front door, but I made no move to answer it. Had I ordered food? I might have. The days were kind of blending together.

The knob started to turn, and the faint click of the dead bolt sounded through the living room. Jared stepped through the doorway, looking irritated. It wasn't the first time he had stopped by to try to drag my ass out of the house. He wouldn't be any more successful tonight.

"What are you doing here, man?"

I gestured to the TV like it was obvious.

"You need to get off this fucking couch and do your job. Eric is swamped right now. *I'm* swamped right now."

He landed on the couch next to me and grabbed the remote. The screen went black before I had a chance to protest.

"I was watching that."

"What's going on with you? You're ignoring me, you're ignoring Eric. You acted like a total asshole to Al at the opening."

"Don't talk about her," I snapped.

"Oh, wow, finally some freaking emotion. That's the most I've gotten out of you in days. I'll talk about her if I want to talk about her. You treated her like trash, in front of all of us. It was a shitty thing to do, and you know it."

"Not everyone wants a pathetic codependent relationship like you and Janelle have."

Jared shoved me, hard, and sprang up. "Watch your mouth. You might be my best friend, but I'm not putting up with your shit. Apologize."

I glared at him before finally breaking eye contact. "I'm sorry," I muttered.

He started pacing the wood floors of my hallway. "I don't get it. Everything was going great for you. Luna Two is shaping up to be a huge success. You finally met someone that you liked. Is this about Al? You seemed pissed at her at the opening. Did she do something? Is that what this is about? Because I know that you really liked her, but no girl is worth blowing everyone off like this."

"I saw my father."

Jared paused mid-step. "When?"

"Last week, right before the opening. When I told you and Eric that I was sick."

"Why did you lie?"

I shrugged. "Because I knew you'd either try to talk me out of it or insist on going with me."

"Damn right I would've."

He sank back down next to me, rubbing his eyes. Even though Jared was the only person in my life who knew my father, I still couldn't bring myself to tell him that I was going to see him. The way my father spoke to me made me feel ashamed. Like all of a sudden, I was a scared little boy and not a thirty-year-old grown man.

"How was it?" he asked after a few beats of silence.

"How do you think? He's the same old bastard he's always been."

"I'm sorry you had to deal with him alone. I know how much he gets to you."

"He doesn't get to me."

Jared hesitated, looking at me, and then back to the floor. "Look, I know you hate talking about this. And I know I'm not the best at talking about deep shit either. But the stuff you went through growing up, the things he's *said* to you...it's messed up." He pulled in a deep breath. "You should talk to someone, like, professionally. I think you might be depressed or something. I can't watch you fade away anymore. I love you, man."

My instinct to laugh and make fun of the idea of therapy was completely snuffed. Was I depressed? I wasn't sure, but I knew I didn't feel like myself.

"Maybe," I finally said, and Jared's face shone with relief.

"That's great. I'm glad you're even considering it. I miss my friend."

We sat in silence for a while longer.

"I fucked everything up with Al," I finally admitted.

Jared chuckled. "Yeah, I think you did."

I glared at him.

"You should apologize. Don't let this shit with your dad get in the way of you finally being happy."

I scratched the back of my neck and tapped my foot. "I don't know. I think I need to figure my issues out before I drag her into anything."

"You don't need to be perfect to let someone in like that. You can work on yourself and be a good partner."

"I think I already friend-zoned her."

"Friend-zoned?" Jared laughed. "That would imply that you two are still friendly. I'm pretty sure you comfort-zoned her. Time to get uncomfortable and call her."

I contemplated this, but I doubted she would even take my call at this point. It had been a week. I wouldn't want to hear from me either.

"But first, let's get your ass off this couch and to your job before Eric kills you."

THIRTY-THREE
AL

"I want to be at a company where my ideas are valued. I want to make a difference." I continued to rattle off a laundry list of what I was looking for in my next position.

Isabel White, the CEO of a women-led tech start-up nodded. This was my final interview, and I desperately wanted to land this job. There were only fifteen people at the company, and the entire interview process made me feel more engaged than I had in my entire year working at my previous company.

An hour later Isabel walked me out and shook my hand.

"Thanks so much for coming in. You'll be hearing back shortly."

I practically skipped outside the building and onto the sidewalk. It was hard not to get my hopes up when during the interview she said she had a good feeling about me.

I shot off a text to our roomies' group chat.

Al: I think I crushed it.

Nora: Yay!!! Go, Al!

Sean: Congrats! Fingers crossed!

Cam: Love that for you!

The smile plastered to my face faltered a little when I saw the unanswered text from Dean still sitting in my messages.

To my shock, he had texted me over the weekend. At first, I had been dying to see what he had to say for himself. My heart dropped all over again when all I saw was a "Hey." After how cold he was to me at the opening and then ignoring me for a week, all he had to say was "Hey"? Screw that. He hurt me, and he didn't care.

Feeling emboldened, I held down the trash icon next to the message. It was time to move on.

Minutes later I was in front of Tiff and Eric's house. I hadn't been here since the night he proposed. Which also just so happened to be the first night I spoke to Dean. *Stop thinking about him,* I scolded myself.

Tiff had been begging me to stop by. We hadn't seen each other since the dreaded opening night, and she thought I'd been avoiding her. I would never admit it to her, but she was right. Feeling the sting of rejection was bad enough on its own. It didn't help that I had witnesses.

But avoiding people I liked because they had ties to Dean was cowardly. When I found out the office I just interviewed at was in Tiff and Eric's neighborhood, I knew I had to reach out and face them. Although I was still hoping Eric wouldn't be there.

Seconds after I knocked, the door swung open and Tiff's blonde curls and bright face greeted me. She threw her arms around me for a quick hug, and I easily returned it. Was it my imagination or had I become way less awkward?

She instructed me to follow her to the kitchen, where she was making us some snacks. Perched on a bar seat, I watched as she chopped an onion and rattled on about how nervous she was about the wedding.

"What happened? I thought you were so relaxed about the whole thing."

"I was. I was." She stopped chopping to look at me. "I think it's the fact that it's *so* soon. I mean, I hardly had time to process being engaged, and now I'm going to be someone's wife?"

I snorted. "That 'someone' just so happens to be the love of your life that you've been dating for five years. You have nothing to be nervous about."

She smiled. "I know, and I guess that's only part of it. I think everyone is at least a little nervous before their wedding. I know it's small and intimate, but I still want everything to go well."

"Is there anything you have left to do? I can help."

"Not going to lie, one of my ulterior motives in inviting you over tonight was to help me make the table centerpieces."

"I'm warning you now, I don't have a single crafty bone in my body. But I'll try my best."

Tiff put the dip she was making in the oven and led me to the living room, where she spilled out a box of ribbons, glass vases, tea lights, and fake flowers. I started to wield the hot glue gun and prayed I didn't burn myself.

"I talked to Jess the other day." Tiff looked up from her vase as she said it, trying to gauge my response.

"Oh?" I didn't want to talk about that. It was bad enough that this Dean situation was hanging over us, I didn't want Jess to come between us too.

"She seems pretty upset that you two are in a fight."

"She's just—she's just so..." I trailed off, not able to come up with a diplomatic enough word.

"So self-absorbed?" Tiff offered.

"Well, yeah. A little. I don't want to trash her, but I don't think she's been there for me lately, and I snapped."

"Look, I don't blame you. I remember even way back when you two were naive eighteen-year-olds. She always had to be the center of attention, and she was happy to have you do all her bidding."

I nodded. "It has always been a bit like that. And lately, I've finally been putting myself out there more. I'm making new friends and figuring out what I want to do with my life. It feels like she wants me to stay the same person I always was—uncomfortable in my own skin."

"I think she's scared that if you become your own person, you won't need her anymore."

"Maybe, but that's on her to figure out. I'm not going to hold myself back to make her feel better."

"And you shouldn't. You were right to say something to her. I'm proud of you."

I rolled my eyes. "Don't get all sappy on me, Tiff."

"I won't, I promise." She resumed attaching a piece of ribbon to a vase. "Do you think you two will make up though? She was your best friend."

"I think we'll be friends again. I hope so at least. It's just going to look a lot different than it did."

A *thunk* sound came from the top of the stairs, and Eric appeared.

Shit. I thought he wasn't home.

He stopped in his tracks midway down the stairs as soon as he saw me. Then he resumed his descent and plastered a smile on his face, trying to act like he didn't just falter.

"Hey, Al. It's been a minute."

"Hey, just helping Tiff be a DIY bride." I smiled and prayed he wouldn't mention Dean.

"These look great." He surveyed our handiwork before placing a kiss on the top of Tiff's head.

"I've got to stop by the original Luna today. I've hardly been there since the open—" He stopped mid-sentence and snuck a glance at me.

Ugh, this was *so* awkward.

"I have to get going. You two have fun."

I felt relief as he opened the front door, but at the last minute, he turned around and mumbled, "He's miserable if that makes you feel any better."

I waved his words off. "You so don't have to say that. It's fine."

He nodded, uncomfortable, and retreated.

After a few beats of silence, I knew I wasn't going to get out of this next conversation with Tiff.

"So, about that..." She trailed off.

"What about that?"

"I'm so mad I could punch him." Her calm demeanor was gone. "I asked him—no, *begged* him—to leave you alone, but of course he couldn't. And then right when it seemed like you guys were getting serious, he just blows it."

"It's fine, Tiff." While this was not a funny conversation, I couldn't help but chuckle at her sudden passion.

"No, it's most certainly not *fine*. I even gave Eric a piece of my mind about that friend of his."

"Don't drag Eric into this." My face must have looked horrified because she immediately backpedaled.

"I mean, we *barely* talked about it." She sighed. "I hope you don't feel awkward seeing him at the wedding."

I assured her that it would be fine, but the reality was I was dreading it. He was probably going to bring a date, which made me nauseous to even think about. She would hold him tightly on the dance floor while I looked on from the sidelines.

What if he tried to talk to me? What if he *didn't* try to talk to me? I honestly wasn't sure which scenario would be worse.

"I have a huge favor to ask you." Tiff's voice pulled me from my spiraling thoughts. "My friend's younger brother just moved here, and he hardly knows anyone—" I didn't like where this was going. "I told her I have this great single friend, and we were hoping the two of you might be able to hang out this weekend."

My instinct to say no was intense. But then I thought, why not? If the Dean situation had taught me anything, it was that I was ready to meet someone. Ideally, someone that wanted me back.

"Sure, why not?"

Tiff squealed at my response and pulled out her phone. "That's amazing. Let me show you his picture. He's so cute." She winked at me. "Hey, maybe if it goes well, you can bring him to our wedding."

"I think you need to reign in your expectations."

THIRTY-FOUR
DEAN

"Thanks again for meeting me here." The gorgeous raven-haired woman standing next to me pursed her lips as we waited for the host to seat us.

"It's not a problem."

"I would normally have come to you, but this is closer to my daughter's day care, and I have to grab her right after this."

"Of course, and sorry again that Eric couldn't make it. He's getting married next week, and he's been running around like a madman trying to get all the last-minute details in order."

She laughed. "A new restaurant and a wedding in the same year? That's quite the overachievement."

Lucy was our new representative from the investment group. After the opening, Eric and I had several disagreements with Todd. One was that I finally gave him a piece of my mind regarding what he said about Al at the BBQ. Eric ended up lodging a formal complaint, and it turned out that we weren't the first people to do so. They immediately replaced him with Lucy, who, from what I could tell, was humble, intelligent, and much easier to work with.

We were meeting over dinner to go over some financials. Normally, Eric would be doing this, but, like I said, madman.

My eyes danced across the restaurant before catching sight of a petite brunette in a green sweater that made her skin glow. I froze. After weeks of not talking, seeing her again felt like finally being able to take a deep breath after swimming underwater. She pushed her chair back and rose from the table she was at.

Realizing she would have to walk right by us to leave, I started panicking. I had fantasized about this moment so many times, yet still hadn't come up with the right words. I was still rehearsing in my head when I noticed that she wasn't alone. A boyish-looking guy was leading her toward the door, his hand on her lower back. He said something that made her laugh. That pissed me off.

At that moment, her brown eyes met mine, and her smile dropped. She glanced between Lucy and me before averting her gaze to the floor. She brushed by me with her date without saying anything. I clenched my fists and knew I couldn't let her go like that.

I apologized to Lucy and told her I had to step out for a few minutes. Rushing outside, I looked both ways before seeing the two of them waiting at the end of the block. All of my beautiful, apologetic words flew out of my mind as I stalked toward them.

"Hey!" I yelled. "Wait up!"

Al looked uncomfortable as I approached them.

"Can I talk to you?" My question came out more like a demand.

She sighed, as if even seeing me was draining her energy. She turned to her date without responding to me.

"Sorry, I should probably talk to him. Thanks again for dinner. I'll text you, okay?"

The guy looked at Al and then back at me, unconvinced. "Are you sure? We could split a taxi or someth—"

"She's fine." I stepped between them and crossed my arms.

Al rolled her eyes at my display. "It's really fine. Thanks though."

He nodded, still looking unsure, but he finally crossed the street and headed off into the night.

"What was that about?"

I turned around to find Al staring at me. Her posture could not have been more closed off, with her arms crossed and her body turned half away from me. I put my hands in my pockets to actively force myself not to reach out to her.

"I just want to talk to you." My macho act felt dumb now that it was just the two of us.

She scoffed. "Now you want to talk to me?"

"I guess I deserve that."

"And I deserve someone that doesn't sleep with me, treat me like shit in front of his friends, and then pretend like I never even existed." She raised a finger with each tick she had against me.

I winced at her words. Now that we were face-to-face, I couldn't ignore how badly I had hurt her.

"I'm sorry," I whispered.

Even though cars were buzzing behind us, the street felt silent as I waited for her response. She wouldn't meet my eyes.

"It's fine. You should get back to your date."

"That's no—I'm not on a date. She works fo—"

"You don't owe me an explanation."

"I promise you I haven't even thought about anyone else." I hesitated before pressing. "Who the hell was that guy anyway?" I knew this was the wrong thing to say in this moment, but I couldn't help myself.

"It's none of your business."

"Are you dating him?" My anger was rising even though I knew that the only person I had to be angry with was myself.

She flung her arms in the air in agitation. "This was our first date, if you must know."

"And the last?" I asked hopefully.

She glared at me.

"You never texted me back," I probed.

"You're unbelievable. You tell me you have no feelings for me after sleeping with me. Then after a week of ignoring me, you just write, 'Hey'? What the hell am I supposed to say to that?"

I shrugged. This conversation had gone better in my head.

"You need help." Her eyes glistened, and I knew that she was fighting back tears.

I took a step toward her, but she backed away.

"I'm getting help," I murmured. "I started going to therapy. It's going okay so far."

A tear fell from one of her eyes before she brushed it away. Her eyes softened a bit before she put her guard back up.

"If it's going so well, then why are you harassing the girl you don't have feelings for and chasing her date away?"

I held my hands up. "Hey, I said I started therapy. I didn't say I was an overnight success story." I smirked, praying to God that she still found me at least a little bit charming.

"Well, I'm happy you're working on yourself."

This was the part where I was supposed to tell her that I did have feelings for her. That I hadn't stopped thinking about her. That my biggest regret to date was how I treated her that night. But her chilly demeanor made me falter.

Instead, I said, "So are you still going to Eric and Tiff's wedding?"

"Of course I am. She's my friend too, you know?" She scowled at me. "I need to get out of here."

"Al, wait." I took a step forward and reached for her.

"No." She put out her hands as a barrier between us. "You hurt me, Dean. I don't know what it is you're trying to do right now, but I can't deal with it. Goodbye."

With that, she turned on her heel and walked as fast as she could away from me.

My heart was beating out of my chest. That could not have gone worse. My shoulders slumped as I walked back to the restaurant. The only thing keeping me from feeling worse was knowing that Al would be forced to see me again next weekend at the wedding.

I promised myself I would be much better prepared.

THIRTY-FIVE
AL

The winding driveway outside of the city seemed to stretch endlessly. My foot tapped against the floor of the back seat of the taxi. Minutes later we approached an enormous white building. Brightly colored flowers lined the front entrance despite the outside temperatures dropping daily.

"Your friends have money with a capital *M*." Cam leaned over me to get a better view of Tiff and Eric's wedding venue.

Yesterday, when I was packing for tonight, I had a mini meltdown about seeing Dean again after our recent awkward encounter. Cam decided I shouldn't have to face this alone and offered to come with me as my plus-one. He claimed he was motivated solely by sympathy and not by the free fancy dinner or open bar.

Once inside with our luggage, I got a distinct feeling that I shouldn't touch anything. Every surface of this place was shiny and polished. Which probably meant I'd wind up breaking something fragile.

Cam threw himself on one of the plush white beds the moment we stepped into our suite.

"Mmm," he moaned into the down pillow. "I'm so glad I could be here for emotional support."

"Right. I'm sure that was your only motivator."

The bathroom was ornate with a double sink and a Jacuzzi tub. I spilled my makeup out onto the counter and assessed my face. Normally, I stuck with a pretty natural look, but tonight I wanted to look amazing. The best I'd ever looked.

For Eric and Tiff's wedding, of course. No other reason.

Before doing my face, I made sure to hang up my dress and inspect it for any wrinkles. It was a rust-colored silk shift dress that Nora had loaned me. The dress fit me like a glove and made me look more mature. At least I thought so.

An hour later I emerged from the bathroom, fully made up and donning the dress. Cam was tying his navy printed silk bow tie in the mirror and saw me approach in its reflection.

"Damn, you look hot." Cam signaled for me to do a twirl. "Someone is going to regret their choices tonight."

I hoped so.

"You may now kiss the bride."

Eric dipped Tiff's head back and kissed her sweetly while the intimate crowd cheered. They both held their hands up as if in victory and started heading back up the aisle.

Tiff looked radiant. Her blonde hair was curled softly and pulled back into a low bun. The lace dress looked like it was made for her. It hugged her figure before flaring out at the bottom into a dramatic train.

Their ceremony was short and sweet. Although I tried to give them all of my focus, I couldn't help but find the tall groomsman in the front with the messy hair and killer shoulders a little distracting. He looked amazing in the black suit he was wearing.

Stop that.

I scolded myself for feeling anything toward Dean. It was hard to convince myself that I was over him.

As if reading my thoughts, Cam leaned in to whisper into my ear. "Okay, seeing him in *that* suit must hurt."

"Not helping."

The wavy, dark head of hair turned abruptly, and I was met with clear green eyes. My cheeks burned, and I jerked my head down, feeling guilty for being caught staring. Meanwhile, Cam wiggled his fingers at Dean, giving him a small wave. I grabbed his arm and forced it down.

"What do you think you're doing?" I hissed.

"What?" He laughed. "Might as well have some fun with him."

"Just play it cool."

The crowd started filing out to the cocktail hour that we were instructed to go to in the lounge area just outside where the ceremony took place.

A server held out a tray with glasses of champagne. I eagerly took one and downed it without hesitation.

"Where'd he go? Do you see him?" My head whipped around, searching the crowd.

"So glad we're playing it cool."

"Hey, Al." My pulse sped not at Dean's voice, but Jess's.

Spinning around, I came face-to-face with her in a bubblegum-pink strapless dress.

"Hey, Jess." I glanced around. "Where's Tom?"

"Oh, he's trying to flag down the one server that had pigs in a blanket."

"Charming." Cam gave her a smile I knew to be fake.

"Oh, you must be Cam. I'm Jess."

Cam shook her hand. "Yes, I've heard *so* much about you."

Jess rocked in her high heels, looking uncomfortable. "How are you?"

"She's great. She got a new job. A fantastic job."

I eyed Cam, silently signaling him to let me handle this.

"You did? That's so great."

It *was* so great. After my interview with Isabel, I heard back the next day with an offer. It wasn't quite as much as I was making before, but I would be somewhere I was respected and excited about what I was working on.

"Thanks. I start next Monday. I'm just glad to finally have a fresh start."

"Congrats." Jess knit her forehead. "Listen, I know that this is Tiff and Eric's day. I just wanted to come over here and hopefully make things less awkward. I want to have fun tonight, with you. And then maybe we could have dinner next week?" Her eyes looked more sincere than I'd ever seen them. "I miss you," she added.

I squeezed her arm. "Let's do dinner next week. And let's have fun tonight."

She grinned. "Really?"

"Yes, find me when our song comes on."

She gave me a nod and a smile before leaving us.

"That was big of you." Cam's voice dripped with disdain.

"Hey, be nice. She was my friend for years. It would be nice to get some sort of relationship back."

"All right, ladies and gentlemen, please find your seats." Jared was speaking into the microphone that was located at the front of the dance floor. His band's equipment was already set up behind him. "Get your glasses ready. It's time to toast the beautiful bride and groom."

Tiff's father came up briefly and thanked everyone for

being there. Again, I tried my best to listen, but I was too distracted. The head table was on display for everyone to see, and I was actively trying not to make eye contact with Dean.

After polite applause and cheers, Jared took back the mic.

"All right, everyone, now we're going to hear from the best man. Dean, take it away."

My heart stopped as Dean stood up and took the microphone. He smiled at everyone and pulled out a piece of paper.

"I'm aging us by saying this, but I've known Eric for almost half of my life at this point. In fact, we met at this exact country club. I wish I could say that I was the most significant person that he met here, but unfortunately for me, I think that title goes to Tiff."

Some chuckles erupted in the audience.

"When we met, we were still young and had shitty attitudes. We would go on joyrides in the golf carts after the club had cleared out—if anyone in charge of this place heard that, I swear it was all Eric's idea." More laughter. "A lot has changed since then. We've gotten in a few fights, opened a couple of restaurants." There were a few small cheers from the guests. Dean smiled. "And we've even fallen in love."

It seemed like he was looking at me when he said that, but I dropped my gaze to my hands.

"As soon as Eric met Tiff, I knew that it was over for him. She wears her heart on her sleeve and is the most genuinely kind person I have ever met. If anyone knows me, they know that I'm a bit cynical when it comes to love and relationships. But these two—among other things—have made me a believer."

"Ouch." Cam was squeezing my wrist at this point, and I was about to lose circulation.

"To Eric and Tiff." Dean raised his glass, and there was no question now that he was looking directly at me.

"He's looking right at you," Cam breathed next to me.

"I have eyes," I snapped.

I wasn't sure how I expected Dean to act toward me today, but staring at me during his heartfelt toast was definitely not it. Our last interaction was strange, and I hadn't heard from him since. I could lie to myself all I wanted, but I knew that I wasn't over him.

To my horror, I felt tears prickling at the back of my eyes.

Get it together, Al.

"I'm going to find the bathroom," I whispered to Cam, who was already digging into a salad they had delivered to our table.

Weaving through the white linen-clothed tables, I made my way to the large glass doors that led back into a hallway. Once there I leaned back against the wall and closed my eyes. Taking several deep breaths, I tried to steady myself.

I felt his presence before I opened my eyes.

"Are you okay?"

I peeked one eye open to see Dean standing about five feet away from me, looking concerned.

"Yep, I'm fine. Totally fine." I squeezed my eyes shut again. "Just a little dizzy from the champagne."

"Are you *crying*?" he asked, horrified.

Shit, I was busted.

"Fine, maybe I am." I wiped my eyes delicately on my wrist to avoid any damage to the makeup I had spent forever on.

"Why?" Dean probed.

"Because." I looked at him, exasperated. "You're not as easy to get over as I am, okay?"

He took a hesitant step toward me. "I don't know what gave you that idea."

"You," I exclaimed. "You gave me that idea. You don't have the same feelings that I have for you, remember?"

He winced as I threw his words back at him. "Can we talk?"

As a response, I just stood there and stared at him.

"All right, I'll talk, and please...please hear me out." He rubbed his hands together and took a shaky breath. "I miss you, a lot. You need to know how miserable I've been these past few weeks."

"Oh, I'm so sorry that *you* were miserable." I glared at him, but I could feel the hard exterior around my heart cracking at his words.

Keep it together.

"I deserved that. Look, I'm so sorry for how I treated you. When I saw you last week, I should have begged for your forgiveness. Instead, I acted like some jealous idiot." He took another step toward me. "I was scared. After I went and saw my father, I felt like shit. And then seeing you at my opening, being all supportive...it made me shut down. I didn't feel like I deserved it, so I pushed you away. It was so stupid, and I've regretted it every second."

My shoulders slumped at his vulnerable words. "Thanks for apologizing."

"Please, can we start over?"

It was hard to resist him when he was being charming like this. But his actions still stung, and I wanted something real.

"Look, I appreciate you apologizing, and to some degree, I get why you acted the way that you did. But it still sucked."

"Can we please get past this? I'll do anything."

He seemed to be in pain about all of this, and it made my heart soften a little. Maybe we weren't meant to be together, but I was sure I would still see him around. It would be better if things weren't awkward.

"Look, consider this water under the bridge. I don't want things to be weird between us if we run into each other again."

He sucked in a breath and moved a step closer. "I don't

want to just 'run into each other.' I want to go back to how things were—I want you in my life."

The tears were forming again, and I took a shaky breath. "I can't deny that I really like you, but I know now that I can't do casual. I want to be with someone that's sure about me."

"Can that someone be me? I'm *so* sure about you." He took another step forward until we were practically touching.

"You cutting me out of your life showed otherwise. I can't deal with that pain again. I'm just starting to get over you."

"*Please* don't get over me. I promise I will not be leaving you again. Trust me, I can't take it." He gave me a half smile and looked down at his feet. "I know I have issues, but I'm working on them. And now I know that I actually do have a lot to offer someone—I have a lot to offer you." He reached out and hesitated before grabbing my hand. "As for casual, I don't want that either."

"You don't?" My breath hitched.

"It's hard to be casual when I think I'm in love with you."

His green eyes burned into me.

"You ar—"

Dean cut me off by capturing my lips with his. He cupped my face in his strong hands and kissed me deeply. I kissed him back, no longer able to resist him. After a few moments, he released my mouth but stayed close, keeping his forehead pressed against mine.

"Just so we're clear, I want you to be my girlfriend."

I let out an astonished laugh.

"Well?"

"I guess we could try that whole relationship thing out."

"I think I'm going to be an amazing boyfriend." His lips traveled down to my neck.

Music floated down the hallway, and I was reminded that the reception was still in full swing.

"Do you want to dance?" I asked breathlessly.

"I can't think of anything I'd rather do more." He grabbed my hand and grinned at me devilishly. "Maybe later I can show you my suite."

The smile on my face was huge as I let him lead me back toward the crowd.

EPILOGUE

Dean

"Can you shift a little more on your side?"

"Shift *where*?" Al shouted back.

"To the left."

"Whose left?"

Al dropped her end of the mattress and looked at me exasperatedly.

"All right, you two, enough with the arguing. Let me help." Cam squeezed between the mattress and the door to help Al out on the other side.

"Ready?" I asked.

"Yes," they both called in unison.

I hoisted my side up and heard a thud on the other end.

"What was that?"

"I wasn't ready," complained Al. It sounded like she was on the floor.

Laughing, I set my side down once again. We were never going to finish this. It was hard to believe a year had passed since the first time the two of us had argued over moving a mattress. Now I was helping her take that same mattress to a donation center because she wouldn't be needing it anymore. Not when mine was way nicer and already at my house, where she would soon be living.

The past year was the best of my entire life. My restaurants were doing great. So great, in fact, that Eric and I were even talking about opening a third location. But the real reason for my happiness was Al. Being with her made me feel giddy and excited about life again. She helped heal parts of myself I didn't even realize were broken.

I was so insanely in love with her it was disgusting. All that shit I had talked about relationships made me look like the biggest idiot ever in hindsight, but I couldn't care less. The best part about all this was that I knew she felt the same way about me.

At one point in my life, I thought I would be a bachelor forever. Now, having Al move in with me was the easiest decision I had ever made. I couldn't wait to share my space with her.

After a few minor arguments, we finally loaded the mattress into the van.

"We should have all hired movers. This is miserable," Cam huffed.

Nora and Sean came outside with boxes of their own and loaded them into a rental truck.

"But it's more fun this way," she chimed.

Nora and Sean were also taking the leap and moving in together. Cam was getting his own place downtown.

"This is kind of sad," Al sniffled. "It's, like, the end of an era."

"Stop, I'm going to cry," Nora wailed.

"I swear to God, you better not get sappy on me this early in the morning," Cam responded.

"We already have plans to meet at our new apartment tomorrow," Sean reminded everyone sensibly.

Al nodded and leaned into me for support. I wiped the lone tear that was falling from her eye.

Even in the short time I'd known her, I noticed such a shift in her. She was so much more confident and sure of herself now. She loved her new job and had already gotten a promotion. She was content with her new friends and the boundaries she had set with her old ones. I couldn't be more proud of her. And I couldn't have felt more lucky that she chose me.

"You ready?" I asked.

She beamed up at me. "Very."

Thank you for reading Comfort Zoned! As an indie author, I appreciate it so much! If you enjoyed this book, please take a few moments to leave a review.

Keep reading for a sneak peek of...

Small towns, new beginnings, and unexpected love.

KEY RIDGE

CHAPTER 1

"Seriously, Garrett, wake up! You're going to be late." I threw a pillow at my boyfriend's head and tried to coax him out of our bed for the third time that morning.

"What time is it?" he groaned.

"Seven fifty-five."

Even though we had been together for eight years and lived together for two, his inability to get moving in the morning still irritated me. He always slept through his alarm, so it was up to me to ensure he got up in time for work every day.

I was a morning person through and through and couldn't relate to his zombie-like demeanor. Waking up early to work out, read, or go for a walk was the highlight of my day.

Garrett finally spilled out of bed and went straight for the tiny bathroom the two of us shared. Once I heard the shower start, I breathed a sigh of relief and returned to the living room to savor one more cup of coffee. Settling into our sectional couch, I resumed working on my crossword puzzle.

A warm breeze hit me square in the face through the window I had left open. Now that it was almost October, the intense and humid heat had at last settled down in Florida. It was a luxury to go outside again and *enjoy* the weather without sweating through whatever shirt I was wearing.

"Hey, Mattie." A damp and shirtless Garrett poked his head out of our bedroom doorframe. "We've got dinner with the crew tonight. You'll probably have to head there straight from work."

My mind worked quickly, scanning through all my upcoming social commitments.

"Tonight? I don't remember you telling me that."

"It's kind of last minute. We're celebrating." Garrett looked at his feet sheepishly and rubbed his short brown hair with a towel. "Will and Lauren got engaged last night."

"What?" I exclaimed, springing up from the couch. Will was Garrett's best friend from the college we had both attended. "But-but they've been together for like five minutes."

"It's been a year, babe. Lauren was really riding on him to propose."

"I didn't know riding someone to propose was an effective strategy." I crossed my arms and glared at him.

"Don't even go there. You know how swamped I am with work. Once I make partner, I'll be able to think about marriage."

My chest tightened in that familiar way it always did whenever marriage came up. The subject of our relationship status was an ever-looming issue between the two of us.

I could recite Garrett's excuses by heart at this point. First, it was "But we're too young." Next, it was "We don't have enough money for a wedding." Now, he had moved on to the "Once I make partner" narrative.

"It's getting old watching friends who've been together a fraction of the time we have beat us down the aisle," I muttered.

He walked over to me and cupped my chin in his hand,

attempting to get me to look at him. I relented and stared back into his blue eyes.

"I love you," he said and planted a kiss on my forehead. "I promise when I do propose, it will be the grandest gesture you ever saw. It will put everyone else's to shame."

"It's not just about the proposal. I want to get married to *you*. I want to start our life together."

"We already have a life together," he responded, turning away from me, and heading back to the bedroom to change.

It was pointless to argue with him anymore about this. I knew I was fighting a losing battle. I should have been more insistent earlier on in our relationship. Once a guy knew he could get away with not asking you after four years or six years, he certainly wasn't going to suddenly have a change of heart after eight.

I walked into our bedroom and shoved past Garrett to get into our cramped bathroom and closed the door. Gripping the side of the countertop, I took a deep breath and scrutinized myself in the mirror.

My long, wavy hair was thick and constantly trying to double in size with the Florida humidity. I fingered a blonde highlight that I had recently added to my light brown hair. I thought it popped against my tan skin, but Garrett had said it made me look high maintenance. My blue eyes were almost as light as Garrett's. When we met in college, I remembered thinking that our future children would look adorable with the blue eyes they were sure to inherit from us. Somehow the thought of children felt further away now at twenty-nine than it did back then at twenty-one.

A soft knock echoed through the tiled room. Sighing, I opened the door to face my boyfriend, or some would say, roommate. He met my gaze with pleading eyes.

"Please, let's not fight, okay." He grabbed my hand and pulled me into his chest. "I love you."

"Who's fighting? Not me." I gave him a weak smile, knowing the argument wasn't worth it. It never was.

"You're the best." He gestured for me to exit the room first and smacked my ass when I passed him. "We need to get going. How many times do I have to tell you we're going to be late?"

"I could use some help with the housekeeping team. They don't respect me and it's causing issues. I have to double-check every room they turn over to make sure they've done a good enough job."

I nodded sympathetically at a property manager I had worked with for years as she rattled on about the latest issues she was facing at one of our resort properties.

"Have you tried setting up a meeting with the owner of the company?" I asked her.

"He keeps giving me the run-around. It's useless. Our old company was so much better."

"Well, we have a contract in place with these new cleaners, so we need to make it work. Their rates were much better, and we're going to close out the year with huge savings. It looks great for our department."

She bit her lip and looked unsure.

"Trust me. It just takes time to build these relationships. You're doing a great job. Keep up the amazing work."

I gave her my brightest smile and continued to reassure her. By the time our meeting was over, I had hoped some of my optimism had rubbed off on her. I was known for my sunny disposition and positive attitude at Brook's Boutique Property Management Firm.

I swiveled around in my plush chair and surveyed the view outside my window. Our firm occupied the twenty-fifth floor of a high-rise. When I got my own office last year, I thought I would never get used to the fantastic view. Sometimes I had to pinch myself to make sure I wasn't dreaming. I had gotten a job here right out of college in operations and had risen through the ranks to Director of Property Management.

Despite my best efforts, my mind wandered back to my conversation with Garrett this morning. If only my personal life was on the same trajectory my professional life was on.

There was a knock at my door before it cracked open, revealing a tall redheaded woman looking disheveled.

"Hey girl, how was your weekend?" she asked, sitting opposite my pearly white desk. Sharon from the finance department was the only person I might consider a friend instead of just a coworker.

"Just the usual. Garrett and I went out to dinner, and I hit up the farmer's market on Sunday. What about you?"

"I went to this cute little pop-up bar on Friday and met the coolest guy. Very starving-artist vibes, but he was so hot. Anyway, we ended up going out on Saturday, and you won't believe where he took me." Sharon rambled on about her adventurous weekend.

I felt a pang of jealousy. She was constantly trying new things and meeting new people. It made me feel like such a dull square. I had lived in Florida my entire life, and the only people I hung out with were my friends from college. I thrived on routine, and my idea of an adventure was trying the new sushi place that had just opened up on our block. I was twenty-nine going on fifty.

Actually, my parents were in their fifties and were more adventurous than I was. They had just gone on a two-week

Alaskan cruise and snowshoed on a glacier. I hadn't even *seen* snow in real life before.

"Do you want to grab drinks after work?"

Sharon's question ripped me from my thoughts.

"Can't. Garrett and I have dinner plans." I chewed my lip before continuing. "His friend Will and his girlfriend Lauren just got engaged."

Sharon sat up straight at the news. "Excuse me. They met, like, fifteen seconds ago."

"I know."

"And didn't you tell me Will was a bit of a player?"

"Yep."

"What the hell."

"Trust me. I feel the same way."

"What did Garrett say about it."

"He said Lauren really wanted to get engaged." I wrinkled my nose as if there was a putrid stench in the air.

She scoffed. "And what about his devoted girlfriend of almost a decade? What she wants doesn't matter?"

"It's fine, really. We're just waiting until we're at a more secure point in our lives." My closed-lip smile felt tight.

Sharon rolled her eyes but didn't press the subject further. I knew that she knew what I was saying was bullshit, but she was kind enough not to point it out. I had cried one too many times over a bottle of wine with Sharon for her to fall for the same excuses I rattled off to everyone else.

"Are you ready for the new client pitch this afternoon?" she asked, graciously changing the subject.

"I was just about to go through the deck again. Did you see pictures of this property? It's gorgeous. It looks straight out of a movie. Almost makes me want to move out to the mountains."

She snorted. "Right, and give up your beach days? Not likely."

"Snow just seems so romantic, though."

I sighed and stared at the pictures of the property I had pulled up. It was located next to a ski resort in Colorado. The Key Ridge Ski Lodge. We managed resorts across the state of Florida and had recently opened our portfolio to other states. The prospective client's town was growing in popularity, but they were having trouble scaling. The property was large, and a huge potential money grab for the winter months. I had to nail this pitch.

"I can picture Mike in a Speedo better than I can picture you in snow."

"You're only saying that because he *did* wear a speedo at last year's holiday party."

We both doubled over, cackling, until a knock at the door interrupted our outburst.

"Mattie." My boss, Mike, stepped into my office. "Are you ready for the Colorado pitch? The clients just arrived from the airport. I know we scheduled the meeting for this afternoon, but they're earlier than expected, and I don't want to keep them waiting."

Just then, a gray-haired woman, maybe in her early sixties, and a thirty-something guy walked past my office. The guy was lean and muscular with dirty blond scraggly hair and stubble. He looked rugged and athletic. Although attractive, the scowl he was wearing and the hard set of his jaw were a turnoff for me. Mysteriously moody was not my type, but he was undeniably good-looking, nonetheless.

Sharon gasped. "Was that Giles Stone?"

"Who?" I asked at the same time Mike nodded.

"His family owns the property. He came with his aunt to hear the pitch." Mike made a move to follow them before turning back to me. "I'm going to go with them to the conference room. Meet us there in five."

With that, he rushed out of the room before I could object.

"Who is Giles Stone?" I asked again.

"He's a professional snowboarder," Sharon whispered despite the subject of our conversation being nowhere within hearing range. "Or was. I think he retired, but he was in the last two Winter Olympics. How have you never heard of him?"

"Oh right, *that* Giles Stone. I'm such a huge fan of snowboarding. I *totally* forgot I have his poster hanging in my room."

Sharon rolled her eyes at my sarcasm. "I'm not a winter sports fan either, but he's gorgeous. There's something extra attractive about a guy that does winter sports."

She came around to my side of the desk and pulled my keyboard toward her. She opened a search engine and typed his name in. Pictures of him filled my screen. They mainly consisted of him in winter clothes contorting his body into crazy positions high up in the air.

I stared at her. "Um, what's attractive about winter sports? You can't even see him underneath all those layers. I can't believe you even recognized him."

She clicked on a picture of him shirtless on the cover of a sports magazine to enlarge it.

"You were saying?" she asked.

"He's okay there, I guess."

"You should read up on him so you're prepared."

"By 'read up' do you mean stare at half-naked pictures? I only have five minutes." I closed the window she had opened. "I need to review this deck one more time. I'm sure snowboarding, or his career, is not going to come up in our presentation."

"If you say so." She walked back around toward my office door. "Hey, if it comes up organically, mind slipping him my number in case he's looking for something to do while he's in town?"

I laughed and tossed a balled-up piece of notebook paper

at her.

"Out."

Sitting across from Giles Stone was different than looking at his pictures online. Sharon was right. He *was* gorgeous. And intense. From the moment I entered the room, his deep brown eyes hadn't stopped searing a hole right into me.

His aunt, Bev, seemed nice enough, but she had a slight edge to her. My hand was still throbbing from her firm handshake. All I could do to hide my nerves was plant a massive grin on my face and pretend I was completely at ease.

"Hello, I'm Mattie," I greeted them cheerily. "How was your flight."

"It was fine. We appreciate you flying us out for this," answered Bev.

Giles just grunted in response.

I extended my hand to Giles, and he eyed it like I had an infectious disease. After a few heartbeats, he engulfed my hand in his and gave it a quick shake before dropping it. I noticed him flexing the hand that had touched me.

"So," I turned to Giles. "Colorado, huh? I've always wanted to visit. Must be a beautiful place to live."

"It is," he replied flatly.

His short remark and hard stare had me on edge. This was not the typical demeanor of potential clients.

"What do you think of Florida? It must be pretty different, huh?" I cleared my throat nervously.

He narrowed his eyes. "Obviously."

Bev nudged his arm before turning back to me with a smile. "It's lovely here. Always nice to be in a tropical climate, even if it is just for a quick trip."

Mike cleared his throat. "Well, Mattie is our director of Property Management. She's put together a great presentation for you. I think you'll find it all very informative."

"Thanks, Mike. I'll just get us started, then." I plugged in my computer and my slide deck appeared on the screen in front of us. "Feel free to stop me at any time with questions, but for now, let's just dive right in."

The first few slides outlined our basic structure. We would place a property manager on-site at their resort to handle all the daily operations. They would manage the housekeepers, order supplies, and go above and beyond to keep guests happy.

"And because your property hasn't been updated in a while, our team will make improvements as we see fit to make the space appealing to guests and ensure we capture as many new customers as possible."

Giles mumbled something under his breath. His presence made me uneasy.

"I'm sorry, what was that?" I asked, my voice dripping with politeness.

"I don't think you, or your team, has the first idea what would make us appealing to our customers," he spat. "Our customers *like* our vintage charm. None of them want to stay in a place with the same aesthetic as a sterile doctor's office." He gestured to the conference room we were sitting in.

My lip twitched as I tried to maintain my smile.

"Of course, sir. I didn't mean that the lodge didn't already possess a certain charm. And we would certainly work to create a feel that would appeal to your customer-"

"Please, spare me." He waved his hand as if to dismiss me. "You're so full of shit."

"Excuse me?" I choked out.

"What would a couple of suits that live in Florida know

about running a ski lodge? Do you even ski?" He crossed his arms.

"Well, no," I sputtered. "But I know a lot about hotels and prop-"

"That's what I thought. I've heard enough."

He stood from his chair and circled around the table toward the exit.

"Giles, please sit down. You're being rude." Bev shot me an apologetic glance as she tried to talk down her nephew.

"No, I'm done here. I'll be outside."

With that, he stormed out, leaving me flabbergasted. While I didn't always nail every presentation, this was undoubtedly the first time I had lost someone's interest within the first five minutes.

At least Mike looked just as shocked as I felt. A sure sign that it wasn't my pitch that was the problem. Just that the person I was pitching to was an asshole.

"I'm sorry about him," Bev said, rising from her chair. "It's not you. He's got other things going on."

"It's not a problem," I responded through gritted teeth. It most certainly was a problem. I had spent days on this pitch, and he never intended to listen to it—the nerve of that jerk to waste my time.

"Look, despite that scene he just caused, I'm the decision-maker, and I'm drowning."

My ears perked up at her desperate tone. Was there still a shot of landing this?

"We would be happy to step in and take some of that burden off you," I chimed in. "Trust me. This is exactly the type of work our firm was made for. We'll step in and organize all your processes. When we're done, I promise we'll have your lodge running like a well-oiled machine."

I slid a packet of papers toward her.

"Maybe you and your nephew would like to review our numbers and mission privately to see if we'd be a good fit. I've outlined the details here."

She nodded.

"I appreciate a prepared woman." She winked at me.

Mike was sitting so far forward in his seat that I thought he might fall out of it. I could tell he was eager to intervene, but he knew I had a way of reading people. Bev seemed like the type of person that valued her privacy and didn't like to make a production of things. The raw numbers and no bullshit information were precisely what she needed to make a decision.

She took my packet and paused in the doorframe. "I'll review this on our flight home and get back to you. Again, I'm sorry for the outburst and I hope we can move past this if we do decide to go forward."

"Of course," Mike and I said in unison. I'm not sure which of our smiles was bigger.

As soon as Bev was out of earshot, Mike raised his hand, and I gleefully high-fived it.

"What a save. I thought we were screwed when he walked out of here like that. Good job having that write-up prepared."

"We're not in the clear yet." I reminded him. While I was an eternal optimist, I did try to keep a realistic perspective on things.

"When she sees those estimated returns and reduced working hours, it'll be a no-brainer."

"Fingers crossed," I replied. "Let's just hope if we do land this account, there will be minimal interaction with that pro snowboarder asshat."

ABOUT THE AUTHOR

Allison Speka is a long time reader of romance and first time author. She met her partner in Chicago before they both picked up and moved to Colorado five years ago.

instagram.com/allisonspeka
tiktok.com/@spekaallison